The Story of Singing Waterfall

1

I found myself going back in time, the process of regression being quite similar each time. You count backwards or forwards, you get yourself into a stage of relaxation of various kinds, and then you find your mind going back, back to another time, a time before you were born.

You are instructed to go to a white room that is peaceful, a place that will take you to another time before you were born, as you slowly drift away from this life and take on another identity, find yourself in another skin, as another person and in another time and place.

Go backward, go backward, go backward, you are feeling very relaxed as you close your eyes and find your way back to the past, a world centuries before, a world that is both familiar yet different, a place you recognize on some deep level as a place that you came from and that you could always somehow go back to, even if only briefly.

That was when I opened my eyes.

Suddenly you are no longer on the couch in your living room going into a deeper and deeper state of relaxation, you open your eyes and you are now in the forest of ancient America, an America before the coming of the white man and the genocide that would follow, although your past self didn't know that, they don't know what you know, so you are seeing the world through their eyes.

As I looked around I could see in all directions there appeared to be forest, forests thick with trees like you wouldn't see in the modern world. In every direction was more forest, as far as the eye could see, and the eye could see rather far, not being obstructed by modern-day pollution.

This was from a time and place before deforestation had happened on a large scale. You can feel and taste the air; it is a cleaner air than the air that you find in this time and place. It is a world that seemed more innocent, more pure, somehow, and in a lot of ways more alive.

I look down at my body and see that it is different than my current day body, healthier and more attractive, a different sex and a different skin color, but feeling familiar as one that I inhabited, albeit a long time ago. I can feel my skin is smooth but covered in tattoos that I lack in the current life.

I can feel my breasts and my hair going long down my back and blowing in the gentle breeze I find myself in in this verdant forest I see around me.

There is a feeling of peacefulness and contentment, this place feels like home, and in that time and place, in that life, it was home.

As I looked around and surveyed the village around me it looks rather large, but still small by contemporary standards. But for that time and place it was a reasonably large village, full of life and full of activity, and as I look around I start hearing the sound of drums beating, as it is a festive season.

Women are walking back to the village carrying maize on their backs, it was a good harvest this year and we did not have to worry about going hungry. The village was in celebration to celebrate the coming of the harvest, only one of many festivals, for this was a very festive culture.

There is something that was lost to the modern world, something about the simple joy of being at one with nature, living in harmony with it instead of in opposition to it. The people depended on the food of the land that they could grow themselves and what they could hunt and fish and gather.

This was just one of many many festivals, with a different festival for every season and occasion, to celebrate the simple joy of life and being alive, the simple pleasures of life such as adequate food, clean water and a place to live and call your home.

As I walk through the village, I looked down and find that my feet are bare, they aren't always so, but at this time of year it's more comfortable to have nothing on your feet, to feel the ground beneath you with nothing between you and the earth below.

Children run up and down yelling in joyfulness and playfulness. There isn't a sense of fear in this place, you can see that people trusted one another, the people celebrated together, that the village raised the children instead of the individual, because the future of the youth was the future of everybody and everybody did their part.

I walked down the street holding the hands of my brothers and sisters, much younger than me, this being one of their first festivals that they are likely to remember, so hopefully it will be a good one, just one of very many to come that they will enjoy over the course of their many years.

The village shaman gathers around a fire and does a ceremonial dance as the drums continue beating, hopefully they will scare away the evil spirits who might malign the village, and encourage the good spirits to want to dance and sing and celebrate with the people of the village.

People gather to dance; I dance with many people, brothers, sisters, men, women and children. Everybody has come out for the occasion, the young, the old, several generations all coming together to celebrate the new season and the fruitful harvest, to celebrate the fact that we do not have to worry about going hungry when other tribes might not be quite so fortunate.

Some of those less than fortunate tribes might try to take from us what we obtained through hard work and good fortune, but we do not want to think about that now, we simply want to celebrate our own good fortune while we can.

After the ceremony to thank the spirits of our ancestors for the fruitfulness of the current harvest, we all sit down and we pass around various different forms of food, the first meal of what will hopefully be a season of good and filling meals.

I take a bite of the squash and I feel that it tastes fresh and ripe as I pass pieces of it around to my brothers and sisters, who also taste of the food of the new harvest.

The women come from the fields bringing basket after basket of maize, as the men come back from their hunt bringing deer and other animals to be cooked over the fire. Many men and women come gathering baskets full of fish, the rivers were filled abundantly, for which we all gave thanks at the festival.

As the meal continues we move on and progressed to eating the meats, which taste juicy and fill the taste buds with joy.

The village shaman stands over the fire and blesses the food and joins everybody in a prayer as we sing to our ancestors. I sing loudly and proudly, my voice having a perfect pitch, as all eyes start falling upon me as I sing the ceremonial song. It was a great honor to do so as now I was considered to be an adult by the tribe, so this was a very important festival for me in that regard.

My father, Running Deer, looks at me with eyes beaming with pride, the apple of his eye. I was his oldest daughter, and the fact that I had now reached maturity and was taking a more active role in the ceremonies of the tribe was a source of great satisfaction for him.

He motions for me to come up as he makes ceremonial marks upon my face and arms to signify my entrance into adulthood as everybody in the tribe dances and claps.

"My daughter is now of many summers and soon it will be time for her to have children of her own and to find a good match for her," he said causing me to blush.

The idea of having children was not something I had thought about myself. I enjoyed be spending time with my brothers and sisters and watching the other children in the village, but I had never thought about the idea of actually having and giving birth to children of my own.

"So it is with each generation leading to the next in an unbroken chain, with our ancestors watching over us and ensuring that we have good times and good harvests, to which we give thanks by renewing life with each subsequent generation that we produce, so that there will always be somebody to remember those who came before us."

I stood up there in front of the village and the many elders who all smiled and clapped. My grandmother seemed to be saying something to my grandfather; she had lived for many many summers and was a wise woman, in the same sense that my grandfather was a very wise man. When two wise people were conversing like that it was always of interest what they were talking about.

I want to listen in but all of the clapping and chanting and dancing were too loud for me to hear them. Whatever wisdom they had to share I had no doubt that I would hear it at some point later, if I was meant to hear it at all.

I remembered when my grandmother would use to take me on her knee and tell me about all of the different animals and spirits and all about the ancestors that she remembered from generations back. She had a long memory, a longer memory than most, her old age not diminishing it in capacity in any degree, the same with my grandfather. They could reminisce for hours about the many generations of people that had passed, who had come and gone, whose names they still remembered all of these years later and honored with every action that they took.

That was when I noticed that Angry Elk was looking over in my direction and smiling. I had never noticed him looking at me like that before, but as people have been telling me I was an attractive woman, and many people in the village had taken notice of that fact as I developed into an adult.

My friends pointed and laughed as he waved and looked at me and I waved back, feeling somewhat self-conscious over the fact that I knew he was looking at me, looking at me with a man's eyes like that.

Angry Elk was one of the largest hunters and warriors in the village, known for his savagery in combat and the large amount of game that he would bring back when the men went hunting. Many would frequently say that he was built like a tall and mighty house, or a tree that you could not budge.

He was a stubborn individual, very used to getting his own way in any type of situation, often through his sheer force of will. Everybody would always celebrate when he came back from the hunt because they knew that they would be eating well that night.

Today was no different, he had managed to successfully bring back more game than anybody else in the hunting party, and for that he was given an important role at the ceremony with everybody singing his praises.

I had never noticed him looking at me like that before; frankly I found it a little bit intimidating. Although there were lots of women in the village who would go head over heels for him, something about him always came across as rather imposing, as though just standing in his presence was to be living in his shadow, his actual shadow being quite large in and of itself!

He was a cheerful sort, but he got his name because when he was angry his rage was without parallel, it was downright frightening, and he would rampage like a wild animal and anything that was in his path would get trampled, that is why few wanted to cross him.

I got my name, Singing Waterfall, because many felt that my voice, that my singing voice, sounded as tranquilizing as the sound of a waterfall.

In a lot of ways we were quite opposite, him being a powerful and unstoppable force of rage, me being a calming influence to those around me.

"I think that Angry Elk has eyes for you," my friend Sprinting Rabbit said as she poked me in the side with her elbow and smiled.

I didn't quite know if I wanted him to have eyes for

me in that sense. As I said we were quite different, very opposing personalities, and I didn't quite know him very well. Sure everybody in the village knew him by reputation, but he was sort of a quiet and solitary individual, someone who people respected, but that few knew very well.

For a moment it looked like he was going to come over to me and I didn't know exactly what to say. He wasn't exactly known to be a great conversationalist, being the strong silent type, but when he spoke people tended to listen because his voice spoke of authority.

I decided that I wouldn't let him intimidate me, but at the same time I didn't really want to risk a confrontation, so I started running off with my friends before my father waved me over as he was standing there with Angry Elk.

I knew whatever he wanted me to come over to talk about was most likely important, but at that moment I wouldn't have quite imagined just how important or why, but I would find out soon enough.

2

I went over to my father who had a big smile, he was practically beaming at me, I couldn't remember the last time I had seen him so happy and so seemingly pleased with himself.

"Hello father, hello Angry Elk," I said as I approached the two of them. I had never seen my father together with Angry Elk before, and I was wondering why they were together right now.

"This is my daughter Singing Waterfall," my father said as I shook hands with Angry Elk, which was the first time we have ever had physical contact with one another that I could recall. "She has become an adult now and perhaps you have noticed her around the village."

Angry Elk nodded. "Yes I have seen your daughter many times, her voice is rather soothing, she is an excellent singer."

I had to admit I felt a little bit self-conscious and was probably blushing over the fact that I was getting a compliment like that. I always felt sort of embarrassed by receiving compliments like that, particularly from men in the village like that. I never really thought that my voice was anything special but many others have told me otherwise.

"Thank you," I said, not exactly sure what to be saying to this person who I had hardly exchanged any words within the past. Although I knew him by reputation, and although he knew who I was, I don't think that we had ever had a full conversation before.

As I had already said I found him somewhat intimidating, by his mere presence. I think that most people in the village felt that way. Most of the men in the village knew that they could not best Angry Elk in a fight or in a hunt or in any forms of combat or athleticism, and most women knew that if he wanted to have his way with them he would have his way with them, although many actually hoped for that.

As I looked at Angry Elk up close for the first time I noticed that he had many more scars than I had ever noticed. I knew that he had many scars from being in many battles with many other tribes, but his whole body practically was covered with scars, the sign of a great warrior, but personally I did not find scars to be attractive, scars were the sign of a person who is accustomed to violence, and I was not accustomed to being around people who made violence a way of life.

"I can see that you are staring at my many battle scars," Angry Elk said once again making me feel self-conscious, I didn't really think that I was staring, but I guess that I must have been, and it must have been really obvious, another cause of embarrassment.

"Yes he has been in very many battles and he has won all of them, his many scars attest to the fact that he is a very brave and triumphant warrior," my father said, once again seemingly beaming with pride at this individual who I hadn't had any previous relationship with.

"I can remember every single battle that gave me every single scar," Angry Elk said as he pointed to himself. "Every injury has a story in and of itself."

"Yes, my grandmother often says that every mark has a story behind it," I said feeling sort of awkward and uncomfortable with this line of conversation. I was not really very interested in discussing the how-to's of how he obtained each specific injury. The way I saw it if he was a really great warrior maybe he would have avoided getting those injuries in the first place, it almost made me wonder how many times you had to be injured and how many scars you had to have before you started to learn to try and resolve your differences more peacefully.

"I am very proud of my battle scars, each one is a badge of honor," Angry Elk said as he pounded his chest, once again which was filled with scars. As I looked at all of those scars on his body I started wondering how he managed to survive so many injuries without dying, not that I wanted him to die or anything like that, it just seemed like fate was very much on his side.

"Angry Elk has survived more battles than anybody else his age, he may be young, but he has the old soul of a warrior," my father said as Angry Elk stood there smiling and looking rather prideful. Perhaps he had good grounds for being prideful, he really was perhaps the best warrior in the village, but he always had a way of letting people know that, and personally I always found that a little bit of humility went a long way towards making a person more well-rounded.

"Yes I can see that," I said, not exactly sure how my father wanted me to react to all of this or why he called me over to start having this line of conversation.

"We have heard word that some of the other tribes who have not been so blessed and so fortunate this harvest season might try something, so the other warriors and I are preparing," Angry Elk said as my father nodded in agreement, as though they were telling me some type of secret among men that I was perhaps not previously in the loop about, and that for some reason they were sharing with me now.

"Well I certainly hope that that is not the case, I thought that we had a good thing going with most of the tribes in this area, I thought that we had been getting along rather peacefully with them," I said suddenly feeling nervous as to why they were sharing this information with me.

"That is why I am hoping that if the village does come under attack that Angry Elk here will be able to lead the warriors in a triumphant battle to protect us, to protect you," my father said suddenly making this all very personal. Why was this about me all of the sudden?

"I have no doubt that he will be able to, but hopefully it will not come down to that," I said feeling increasingly awkward by the moment. I still did not exactly see where my father was going with all of this.

My father nodded. "But that is why I always want to

make sure that there is somebody who is going to be there and be able to protect you, and a strong warrior like Angry Elk is someone who I feel is up to the task."

"I am sure that that will not be necessary, as I don't feel that I need protecting," I said starting to feel even more uncomfortable with this whole situation, feeling like I was the subject of a conversation where I was not in on all of the facts of the conversation.

"Your father has offered me your hand in marriage," Angry Ek said with a smile as he beat his chest and laughed.

"Marriage?!" I said suddenly taken aback as I realized what they had been getting at. I had never seriously thought about or considered marriage in any major way before, which is probably why I did not pick up on what my father was getting at when he called me over.

My father nodded. "I know that Angry Elk will be a good provider and protector for you, you will never go hungry and you will never have to worry about being safe and protected from outside forces that might do us harm. That is why I felt that the announcement should come here at the festival, tonight is a positive event marking your first festival of adulthood, and that is when you should really be starting to think about marriage in a really serious way."

"I guess I had never thought about marriage before," I said, still not exactly sure how to respond to a situation and an offer like that. I didn't want to hurt Angry Elk's pride, which was considerable, and perhaps more fragile than his strong demeanor suggested.

My father smiled. "I guess I forget that until recently you were just my little girl, but now that you are an adult you have to start thinking about more adult things, things like family and children. Angry Elk actually approached me saying that he was interested in you."

"You are interested in me," I said pointing to myself rather surprised that that was the case, seeing as he had never even spoken to me previously. How could he be interested in me when he didn't really know anything about me?

My father nodded. "Angry Elk has been watching you lately, maybe you haven't noticed, as I noticed that sometimes you have your head in the trees and more focused on the clouds and nature."

It was true that I often found myself out in the forest away from people, and that sometimes I could be oblivious to what was going on around me outside of nature. I think that I understood nature and animals better than I did other people like that.

"I have seen you looking at me a time or two," Angry Elk said, smiling and laughing as my father did likewise.

I felt like that was an unfair assessment, maybe I had looked at him once or twice, but not in the serious way that he seemed to be suggesting he was looking at me. Had I really been so oblivious?

"So what do you think?" my father asked.

I didn't want to say anything that would be insulting to Angry Elk or to my father, who clearly had a lot invested in this, but having never even been in an intimate relationship with others before, and having only recently learned about where other people came from originally, I guess that in my young age and inexperience that I had not really been thinking from an adult mindset.

"I guess I am quite flattered, I really didn't think that anybody was looking at me, like, well like that," I said as my father and Angry Elk both laughed.

"Well I have been, perhaps if you had your head in the clouds less you would have noticed," Angry Elk said with boisterous laughter. For a moment that almost felt like an insult, but I could see that my father was about to come to my defense.

"Singing Waterfall is very in touch with nature, maybe someday she will even become a shaman, she has very well-developed female intuition, but I think that she does spend more time with animals than she does with people," my father said, for seemingly defending me, but now seeming as though he were taking Angry Elk's side, which was making me feel myself on the defensive.

"I like animals as well, although I mostly like hunting them," Angry Elk said with a big belly laugh as my father laughed more, seemingly just going along with him more than being as enthusiastic about it as he was.

"Well anyway I think that perhaps you two to take more time to get to know one another," my father said as he pushed us together. "And a festival is a good social occasion with which to get to know people better."

I felt myself put on the spot, and to refuse would hurt Angry Elk's pride, so I figured that I could indulge him and give him the attention that he was clearly seeking.

"Do you like dancing?" I eventually asked, struggling for topics of conversation.

"I like doing a victory dance when I have completed a hunt," Angry Elk said as I remembered I had seen him do several victory dances before, and he was something of an awkward dancer, not exactly graceful, especially considering that he was such a well-respected warrior.

"Well come on I will try to teach you," I said as I led him over to the center of the village only to realize that all eyes were on us as I began to dance around with him, extremely awkwardly, as he didn't seem to have the slightest clue what he was doing. Again for such a graceful hunter he wasn't equally graceful on his dancing feet.

People in the village started beating the drums as we continued to dance, as well as making other festive noises. I looked over at some of my friends and I couldn't help that they were looking at me, and a couple seemed to be smiling and waving, so I simply waved back, but I could see that a couple of them, like Sprinting Rabbit, were clearly giggling.

I was feeling really self-conscious being up there with Angry Elk in front of the whole village, as though we were somehow together as a couple, but for a moment it wasn't the worst feeling in the world. As I saw my friends looking over in that direction I could see hints of jealousy, so I figured I might as well go with it. I know that several of them would have given their left arm to be where I was, so I wasn't about to throw away this opportunity to make my friends jealous and become the talk of the town.

When we had finally finished dancing, Angry Elk fortunately wanted to go off and talk with the other hunters. I could see him pointing over in my direction and laughing as the other hunters laughed with him. I can only hope that they were laughing with me instead of at me, but the idea that all of these men were paying me so much attention all of the sudden was something I was not accustomed to.

"I can't believe that you were actually dancing with Angry Elk," Sprinting Rabbit said as I came over. "What was it like to be so close to him? Is he actually interested in you?"

I looked over in his direction as he continued to laugh and hold his belly with his friends.

"I think he's interested in something," I said, realizing I think for the first time exactly what he saw in me. He wasn't seeing me as a marriage partner, so much as a woman with a woman's body, which once again made me feel suddenly self-conscious in a way that I hadn't felt before.

"Then I guess the luck of the ancestors is with you," Sprinting Rabbit said once again giggling and smiling.

But as I looked over at Angry Elk with his fellow warriors, looking as though he was already boasting about some type of conquest that never actually took place, I couldn't help but think that maybe luck wasn't the best word to use, and I was going to find things would be increasingly awkward in the days to come.

But for now I decided that I would dance and sing and enjoy the festival and I danced and sung well into the night until I could do no more.

I would sleep well that night.

3

I wasn't expecting that the next day when I woke up that I would be the talk of the town, more or less as a result of having being seen dancing with Angry Elk. I guess I had never thought about my social standing in the community before, as I knew that people found my physical appearance and my singing voice to be attractive, but I never thought that I was considered to be a highly eligible woman around town, and now it seemed like all eyes were on me.

"I can't believe that you are actually potentially going to be married to Angry Elk," Sprinting Rabbit said the next day as we were walking together gathering food in the forest.

"But I barely even know him," I said shaking my head. "In fact I think last night was the most time we have ever spent together and the longest conversation we ever had, and it wasn't even a very long conversation at that. How can one conversation like that be the most you get to know somebody before marrying them?"

"I just know that if I were in your position I wouldn't be questioning things, I would probably be jumping for joy. Angry Elk is the best hunter and warrior in the entire village, he might even end up being chief someday, you could be the wife of a chief, don't you find that to be exciting?"

I shrugged my shoulders. "I guess I never really thought about it like that before, I don't usually concern myself with those types of things."

"Well you should, because now you are the focus of everyone's attention in town. Just the fact that he showed interest in you like that has elevated your social status through the roof, soaring like a bird."

I shook my head again. "I guess I never really thought much about things like social status and everything like that, it was really never that important to me. I don't understand how the attention from one man like that can suddenly get everybody in town focusing on me."

"Really, you don't? When the most important and prominent person in the town suddenly wants to marry you, you really don't understand how that can elevate your social status and get everybody talking about you?"

"But I don't really like being the subject of people's conversations and gossip like that, you know how I like to spend time by myself and not to draw attention to myself."

Sprinting Rabbit nodded. "I've known you longer than anybody, and I know you often go out of the way to be by yourself, and you spend more time with animals than people and like to be in nature and everything, but I think that you have to realize that you are an attractive woman and that people are starting to look at you, you know as a woman."

"Yes I have started to realize that," I said once again feeling self-conscious. I still wasn't used to the idea of people looking at me just in that way. I felt like until recently I was considered an innocent young girl, and now all of the sudden I was an adult, and I was supposed to be thinking about marriage and baby making and things of that nature as my first priority.

"It's just I can't believe that you are taking this so casually, Angry Elk himself is actually interested in you, and you never even noticed that he was interested in you before?"

I shrugged my shoulders once again. "Like I said I never really noticed, maybe my head really is in the clouds all the time. I just never realized that anybody was really looking at me in that way. As I was saying, yesterday at the festival was the most interaction I have ever had with him, and now I am supposed to believe that he wants me for his wife, just out of the blue like that? It's a real lot to take in."

"No denying that, if I were you I would probably be head over heels, I mean me the wife of a chief, the wife of the top hunter in the tribe, I mean haven't you ever, well, you know thought of somebody like that?"

"I guess not, I always looked upon him just like any other guy in the village I suppose."

"Well that's rather ironic, seeing as I think that you are probably the only woman in the village who views him as just another guy in the village. I can't believe that you never realized he was taking notice of you before."

"You never told me that he was looking at me like that, so I'm guessing you didn't notice either."

"Well occasionally I noticed him looking over at you, but then that was when we were together and I guess, well this is a little bit embarrassing, I guess I just assumed, or at least liked to believe that he was looking at me not you, no offense or anything."

"None taken," I said as we both giggled. "I just feel this is all happening so fast, how am I supposed to build a relationship with a man who I barely even know, a man who really never even talked to me until just the other day?"

"Well your father seems to think he is a good match for you, and who can blame him, I am sure that any man would want his daughter to marry the best hunter in the tribe. He is just looking out for your well-being and your future and everything, you really should be thinking more about your future."

"Well I think I have been thinking more about my future in these last couple of hours than I probably have in the whole rest of my life. I have always been living on sort of a day to day basis, I guess I never thought about marriage or children or raising a family like that. To me the creatures of the forest always seemed more like family."

Sprinting Rabbit laughed. "I don't mean to laugh at you, I respect and appreciate the animals and the spirits inside of them just as much as everybody else, but you can't exactly have a family with a deer or a bear or a mongoose or anything."

I smiled. "I suppose you are right about that, but I still like the time I spend in the forest alone. Being a wife,

I don't know, it comes with certain obligations."

"Are you saying that you were never planning to get married or anything like that?"

"I never said that exactly, I'm just saying that I never thought about it until now, and this is all just a lot coming at me at once. I would just like to have more time to think about it is all, it's a big decision."

"I'll say, although if it were my decision I wouldn't have to think about it more than a minute before saying yes, and that's assuming I didn't faint when the proposal was made to me. But I guess that is what makes us different."

"I guess so, but I love you just the same for who you are," I said as the two of us hugged. "Now come on I know where we can get the best berries but it's a little bit further away from here."

We continued to spread through the forest, and Sprinting Rabbit lived up to her name as she was always much faster than me. It seems like whenever we started running through the forest together she was always a couple of paces ahead of me, and that I could never fully catch up unless she would slow down for a moment to wait up for me. She really was as fast as a rabbit, having won every single foot race with every other woman in the village.

Soon we came to the area where I found the berries that I liked so much. I popped a few in my mouth and they tasted fresh and ripe, just perfectly in season. As I was picking the berries and putting them in my basket I couldn't help but think would this change after I was married? Would I then be gathering berries for my husband, cooking him all sorts of meals?

I had to admit I didn't share Sprinting Rabbit's

enthusiasm for the idea of being a housewife, spending my days cooped up inside of the home, waiting on my husband and providing for him. I valued my freedom; I enjoyed the freedom of the forest, being able to commune with nature and the animals, to have silent time to myself. I couldn't picture myself with a bunch of children that I had to watch and care for all the time.

Of course I loved spending time with my brothers and sisters, but at the end of the day my parents would take care of all of the difficult things and I was free to enjoy myself. But I guess now I was becoming an adult, and with that came adult responsibilities and questions about my future, questions that I wasn't quite prepared to answer at this time and place in my life.

As I breathed in the fresh air of the forest I couldn't help but wonder if once I was married I would be able to spend as much time out here in nature. Of course gathering was an important part of adding to our food supply, but most of our food came from farming or from the hunting of the men, which was precisely why people like Angry Elk were so highly esteemed within the village, they brought back the most food and were considered the best providers, so I could see how being married to him wouldn't necessarily be a bad thing in that regard.

However I did value this time spent in the forest, whether alone or with friends. Something about always being at home all the time and tending to a house feels like it would take time away from the freedom of being in nature.

"Look at the deer," Sprinting Rabbit said as she pointed off in the distance.

It was a large buck, looking rather friendly, and I felt like I wanted to approach it. Slowly I went over to the deer and I let it lick my fingers. I knew how to approach animals in such a way as to not startle them and frighten them away.

"It's true that you definitely have a way with animals," Sprinting Rabbit said as she smiled. "But it wouldn't hurt for you to learn to interact more with people. I've been your friend for many years but you can't spend all of your time out here with animals, I am one of the few people that you seem to spend time with because we enjoy this similar time out in the forest together, but you need to be part of the village more."

"So you think that I should marry Angry Elk?"

"Well if you don't I am wondering if he might be interested in me," Sprinting Rabbit said as she started playing with her hair and trying to make herself look more attractive as the two of us burst out laughing. "I'm serious though, this is like the opportunity of a lifetime and you are treating it as though it were just everyday news, as though it were no big deal, when it's probably the biggest deal of your life, perhaps the biggest news around the village in I can't even remember how long."

"You want me to ask him?"

"Of course I don't want you to ask him!" she said as she pushed me playfully. "Come on I will race you to the lake, right by the waterfall that bears your name."

I knew that it was pointless to try and race against her, as she always would end up winning, but I tried every single time, and every single time she always jumped up in victory when we finally arrived and did sort of a little victory lap to really rub it in.

The sound of the waterfall crashing into the lake actually was rather peaceful, so it was good that it was actually my namesake, as I did rather enjoy the sound of the waterfall, the song of the waterfall if you would.

"Let's go for a swim," Sprinting Rabbit said as she began undressing and diving into the water. She soon came up and looked like she was freezing cold as she started rubbing her arms.

"How's the water?" I asked, seeing that it was clearly very cold.

"Why don't you come in and see," she said as she began splashing at me playfully.

I smiled and looked both ways as I slowly slipped out of my clothing before diving in the water and began splashing her, and soon we were in a full-blown splashing fight. This was one area in which I always managed to beat her, it was the perfect revenge for her winning the foot race contest.

"Okay okay, I give, stop splashing," she said as I splashed her one final time as she laughed.

After hiking in the woods all day and working up a sweat it felt nice to feel the cool water against our naked flesh. It was extremely refreshing and was a very freeing sensation. However that day I noticed I felt different, I don't know why, but I kept looking around like I was expecting to see something, or someone, and I kept lowering my body deeper into the water, so that nothing was visible below my neck.

"Hey is something bothering you," Sprinting Rabbit said noticing that I was behaving differently. "Why do you keep your head just barely above the water, did you get bashful all of the sudden?"

"Who me, no of course not," I said still keeping my head just above the water. But it was true, all of the sudden I felt self-conscious around her for the first time. I guess until just recently I hadn't been thinking about my body in those terms, it was an adult body with adult features, adult features that I knew other people in the village were starting to take notice of.

She laughed. "I can't believe that you are actually bashful around me."

"No I'm not bashful around you, it's just I'm," I began saying before stopping.

She smiled wide as I could see she was richly enjoying this. "I know what it is, you're worried that some guy is going to see you, someone like Angry Elk."

"Not true," I said as I splashed her, basically confirming what she had suspected all along. Soon we were again in a giant splash fight and that at least took some tension away from the situation, but it was true that I had never felt self-conscious about my body like this before.

After a while we stopped splashing one another and I couldn't help but get the distinct feeling that I was being watched. Maybe I was just being paranoid, or maybe my self-consciousness had reached a new level that I didn't think was possible before, but I couldn't help but think that we were not alone in the lake.

"Did you hear that," I said thinking that I saw something in the bushes not far away.

"You know, I think I actually did," she said looking serious for a moment before she started smiling and laughing. "I bet it's Angry Elk coming to get a peek at you!"

"Shut up," I said as I splashed her again before we both shut up as we saw the bushes moving, there was definitely somebody there.

The two of us went silent as we let ourselves get deeper into the stream, when all the sudden out from the bushes came the deer that we had seen earlier coming over to begin drinking. The two of us looked at the deer for a moment before we burst out laughing at how we had gotten frightened over nothing.

The two of us smiled as we watched the deer drinking water until all of the sudden an arrow came and hit the deer in the side of its neck causing it to fall over writhing in agony.

We both screamed as that was when we realized that we were indeed not alone, as we saw what looked like three men emerging from the bushes. I could tell from the tribal tattoos on their bodies that they were not from our tribe, they were from the next village over.

"Well well well, what do we have here," the first man said coming over to us. Now I wasn't just feeling self-conscious, I was actually feeling frightened for the first time. These were our tribal hunting grounds and the other tribesmen that we were seeing right now shouldn't be there.

The other two men sort of snickered, as they could tell that we were not wearing anything in the lake. Luckily our heads were now down completely in the water, trying to conceal our bodies as much as possible from these foreign intruders.

"This is the hunting ground of our village you know," Sprinting Rabbit finally said, with me worrying that she was perhaps inviting trouble. Here we were completely naked in the lake and we were being intimidated by three men with weapons, we did not want to antagonize them.

Now I wasn't feeling worried about being embarrassed, I was feeling worried about whether these men were coming to harm us, because why were they trespassing like this otherwise?

"We were chasing the deer and I guess we lost track of where we were, it's no big deal, we are not going to hurt you," the head of the hunting party said, once again smiling and smirking to his two companions, because they both knew that we were naked and defenseless.

At that moment I just wanted to do anything that would get us out of this situation, anything that would rescue us from this situation without further embarrassment. But of course I wasn't about to step out of the water completely naked and start an argument with these men.

"What are you doing on our tribal land," a familiar voice said as I looked up to realize it was the last person I had expected to see, it was Angry Elk.

Angry Elk was accompanied by his two companions, Howling Wolf and Stalking Badger, who were also experienced hunters and warriors who always hung around with him. At least they were equally matched in terms of numbers if a fight were to occur.

"We didn't mean anything by it, and we are going to be leaving now," the head of the hunters said clearly recognizing the authority of Angry Elk, whose reputation traveled far beyond just this village.

"Good, see that you do," Angry Elk said as the three hunters from the other tribe left without even taking the deer away with them, as they realized that to save face they would have to forfeit it, as it was game that was on our land and not theirs.

"Are you girls okay," Angry Elk said looking at us, and that time I knew he was really looking at us, looking at us very specifically as women with a man's eyes and gaze. Now I was definitely feeling embarrassed and self-conscious if I wasn't before.

"We are fine now that you guys came along," Sprinting Rabbit said, clearly extremely embarrassed by the fact that she knew she was naked and that these guys were only a few inches away from her. She was perhaps even more embarrassed than I was because I knew how she felt towards Angry Elk.

"Perhaps we should escort you back to the village," he said as Howling Wolf and Stalking Badger started snickering, because they both knew that we were naked and trying to conceal ourselves. They were pretty much his lackeys, never disagreeing with him or contradicting him in any way, just sort of snickering and nodding in agreement in deference to him all the time.

"Okay, but just please give us a moment of privacy," I finally said, my head still very deep in the water and trying to conceal myself as much as possible. I could see from the look of his eyes that he was enjoying the intimidation that he was giving to us, the intimidation of potential embarrassment.

"So she does talk," Howling Wolf said as the three of them indicated that they would be waiting over in the bushes.

Sprinting Rabbit and I sort of wadded over to where our clothing was and got dressed. Although the men said that they would give us privacy, as I was standing there, completely exposed to the world, I very distinctly could see that Angry Elk was peering over in our direction and that his two companions were likewise smiling, as I held up my clothing to cover myself up before running into the bushes to get dressed in greater privacy.

When the two of us emerged from the bushes fully dressed, knowing full well that they saw us and that we knew that they saw us, we said little on the way home, but the entire way home I was thinking the same thing that I am sure that Sprinting Rabbit was likely thinking as well.

They had seen us and our adult bodies, and they were very much looking at us with men's eyes, and that was a feeling that I knew that I wouldn't soon shake off.

4

I think that more humiliating than being seen naked by Angry Elk was the fact that he and his male friends ended up escorting Sprinting Rabbit and I all the way back to the village, as though we were little children in need of somebody to corral us and bring us back home safely, as though we were helpless and defenseless.

At the same time though I felt like I was somewhat grateful over the fact that they showed up when they did. Who knew exactly what those other men would have done if Angry Elk and his friends didn't show up when they did, the timing was extremely perfect really.

I still couldn't help think that the whole time though that we were walking home that he was probably picturing us as what we look like naked. Once again I wasn't exactly used to being looked at that way by another member of the tribe, particularly by a man. It was sort of a strange and awkward feeling that was making my self-consciousness go through the roof.

It was strange how maybe just a week before I wouldn't have thought the slightest little thing about a situation like that, as I would regularly go swimming naked with other women from the village, and never at any time did I think that anyone was looking at me as a fully developed adult woman, as a sexual being like that.

I don't know if I was quite ready to accept or to

handle that, but it seemed like the world was expecting me to do so, and to do so all of the sudden with no previous experience. I went from a week ago being a naïve girl to now being an adult woman who is getting marriage proposals and has the prospect of marrying the most eligible man in the village.

As we reached the border of the village and everybody saw us walking home with Angry Elk and the other men, people could tell that maybe something was wrong, as usually we would not require an escort back to the village like that, and being escorted like that again made us feel like we were helpless children, as though we had somehow failed to take care of ourselves.

I saw my father at the edge of the village, and normally he didn't ask where I was all the time, but he could tell just from the fact that we were all walking home together that something was off.

"We encountered hunters from an enemy tribe," Angry Elk said before we had even fully returned from the forest as my dad shook his head.

"You girls are very lucky that Angry Elk and the others were there to protect you and that they came along when they did," my father said. "If there are men from enemy tribes who are going around on our hunting ground that is a violation of our treaties, so until further notice I don't want anyone leaving the village unescorted, particularly young women like you Singing Waterfall and Sprinting Rabbit."

"Dad you know that I can take care of myself, it wasn't like that, you weren't there," I began saying as he shook his head. I could tell from that look in his eye, that although normally he would listen to me, I could tell right now he was going into parent mode, concerned that his daughter might have just come to some type of harm if not for the fact that the best hunter in the village just happened to show up at the exact right moment.

"We will talk about this later, right now I think that I should talk with the men and we should decide what to do. But until further notice I think that everybody should stick close to the village, as there might be enemies afoot, and we can't be too careful."

Seeing my father treating me like this made me feel the opposite of the way he was making me feel the other day. The other day he was making me feel more like an adult woman than ever before, now I just felt like I was a little girl again, and not just that, but a helpless infant, and my father couldn't seem to think that I would know how to take care of myself.

"I'm just so glad that you are safe," said my mother, Graceful Bird, as she hugged me. Although I was glad to be back with my mother and my family and everything like that and now was safe, I didn't feel like I was in as much danger as I was a couple of moments ago. In fact as I looked back on the whole situation it was probably unlikely that those men were going to harm us in any major way, they just happened to be hunting a deer and got a little bit off the beaten path and managed to trespass on our tribal lands, probably by accident at that.

I tried to explain to my mother that they didn't even end up taking the deer with them in the end, and she said once again that it was good that Angry Elk and the others showed up when they did. I could tell from the look on her face that she was agreeing with my father, like many of the women in the village she was in awe of Angry Elk and his reputation. Although I was grateful about him showing up at that moment, I still felt uncomfortable about the fact that he was looking at me, that he had seen me naked, and that he was probably looking at me in terms of a flesh being rather than another human being.

When my father came home later that evening after going to the tribal Council with my mother and the other elders of the village he had a frown on his face.

"I am so very glad that you are safe," my father said as we ate dinner later that evening. "This just backs up my feeling that Angry Elk will be a good match for you, you can see he is more than capable of protecting you."

"In case you didn't notice father I don't need protecting, I am not a helpless child."

"You may be an adult but you still have the mind of a child, you still have not been an adult for very long, I have been an adult very long, as has your mother, and your grandmother and grandfather also agree and they have been adults longer than anybody else, in fact longer than the majority of people in this village. You may not think that you need protection but what happened today just shows how you do need protection. We are going to send out hunting parties to patrol the area to see if there are going to be any enemies who might be causing us trouble in the near future. I have asked Angry Elk to specifically watch out for you when I am not in the village. And after everything that has happened today I think that you should marry him as soon as possible."

"I don't have anything against Angry Elk, but I am not sure if I want to marry him, as I barely know him."

"He is a very handsome man, don't you think," my mother said with a smile on her face that I could tell was making my father jealous, and my father was not normally a jealous man, but the fact that his own wife was just as star struck by the idea of me marrying the top hunter in the village was making him so.

"I guess so," I said not exactly sure how to respond.

"You know most of the women in this village would give their left arm and leg in order to be with him," my mother said shaking her head.

"Well I am not most women; I would rather keep my left arm and leg and be able to protect myself, to stand on my own 2 feet."

My mom shook her head. "Your father isn't trying to say that he doesn't think that you can protect yourself, but it's always good for somebody to be married and to have somebody that they can rely on in times of need and in potential times of conflict as we are seeing now."

"Your mother is right, which is exactly why I am going to arrange the marriage as soon as possible," my father said as though it were a done deal. I wanted to defy him, I wanted to challenge him, but looking at him at that moment I knew that now was not the time to do so. He obviously had lots of other concerns on his mind and I wasn't about to give him any more trouble.

Over the next several days in the village the talk of the town went away from being about me marrying Angry Elk to about the possibility that there could be a war soon. Some of the men and women from our tribe met with the men and women of the other tribe to remind them of the mutually agreed boundaries that we had set between our lands, but they could see that many people in the next village over didn't have as good a harvest as we did this year.

"Well that's a problem they will have to take up with their ancestors and the spirits of the forest," my mother said after breakfast one morning. "I feel sorry that they might not have as much food as we do, but that doesn't give them the right to go trespassing on our tribal lands."

"I am sure that they will respect the boundaries now that we have laid them down more clearly," I said. "The other day was just one incident, I don't think we should have to be worrying about preparing for war just yet, do you?"

My father shook his head. "I don't like to have to prepare for war but it's better to prepare for war now than to be caught by surprise. We have been able to maintain peaceful relations with most of the other tribes and villages in the area, but one bad harvest can often make the big difference between keeping a treaty or an agreement and breaking it. People always do terrible things when they are hungry."

"I am sure that we could probably share some of our harvest with the other village," I said shaking my head.

My father nodded. "We have made them a peace offering of some food but that may not be enough. We can only hope that the other tribes in the area are going to be reasonable, and that they are as committed to maintaining peace as we are. I do not think that they want warfare, but again in times of hunger people do strange things, things that they wouldn't otherwise even consider often horrible things. When that happens I just want to know that all of my family is going to be safe."

"Are you sure that I can't go into the forest to go pick more berries?"

My father shook his head. "I certainly don't want you going alone."

"Well I intended to go with Sprinting Rabbit like I normally do."

My father shook his head again. "Two women out

there alone in the forest is not a safe situation, look what happened to you the other day. If you must go into the forest I would like some of the hunters and warriors to accompany you."

My father gave me a stern look and I knew he meant business. Once again I felt like challenging him, but once again I could tell from the look in his eyes that now was not the time to do so.

Already I felt like I was losing my freedom, going from being completely free in a short time to now feeling like I was constantly under the scrutiny of everybody else, that everybody else was trying to decide my destiny for me based on what they thought was best for me. But nobody had asked me what I thought was the best for myself, that's the thing that I found most insulting.

I was beginning to wonder if this is how it would be like to be married, would I constantly be having to do what Angry Elk wanted all the time, constantly be under his supervision, constantly expected to defer to him the way I deferred to my father?

I certainly wasn't very pleased with the idea, but it looked like my father and my mother were both intent to have this marriage go forward as soon as possible.

"It's just that I feel everything is moving so fast, like everything is changing too fast," I said the next day as Sprinting Rabbit and I were helping to gather corn from the harvest.

"Well it's like the old saying goes that nobody steps into the same river twice, life is all about constant change, you just have to go with the flow sometimes," she said.

"I don't have a problem with stepping in a different river; it's just that I sometimes prefer to go to the river that

I know, the river that has always been constant. I am tired of people telling me to just keep constantly going with the flow all the time."

She shook her head. "Well speaking of the river, I don't think that we will be going there by ourselves anytime soon, everybody in the village is talking about the possibility of war."

"But my dad said that the possibility of war was only a remote possibility, that we have made numerous peace offerings to the nearby villages, and that they have said that they respect our boundaries."

"Yes, but can we really take their word for it? Sometimes I think that you are little bit too trusting, people are not the same as animals, people tend to be selfish, people tend to be violent and cruel, not just for the sake of hunting like animals do. When animals kill each other it's always for food, human beings have the capacity to be much worse."

I nodded. "Now you understand why I prefer spending time with animals to spending time with people most of the time."

She smiled. "Well enough about the prospects of war, let's focus on the positive thing, I can't believe that you are going to be marrying Angry Elk, and I can't believe that you aren't more excited about that. I would give anything to be in your place right now."

"Really, do you want to switch places and marry him instead?"

"Why don't you want to marry Angry Elk, I honestly don't understand that."

"Well didn't you feel a little bit weird about what happened the other day, you know when he saw us at the lake, really saw, saw us as women with women's bodies?"

Sprinting Rabbit blushed and sort of turned away from me before turning back. "Well I mean of course it was a little bit embarrassing and everything, but that's the way men tend to look at women, there's nothing unusual about that, nothing wrong with it, and I wouldn't mind him looking at me like that."

"Well I still feel a little bit strange about it, is that the way he's always going to be looking at me when we are husband and wife?"

She smiled. "I would think that that's the way a wife would want her husband to be looking at her, and the way he would want his wife to be looking at him. Sometimes I feel that you really are little bit naïve about these matters."

"So I have been told, and maybe it is true. It's just like I feel like I am still young and that I am not ready to be tied down with a marriage already."

"In times like these it's always good to have a secure marriage like that, somebody to protect us. I wish I was as lucky as you right now, as I don't feel as safe after what happened yesterday. At least when Angry Elk is your husband you won't have to worry about anybody bothering you or challenging you like that, you'll be his and he will be yours and you will be together forever."

"That's the part that scares me, being forever with a person that I know almost nothing about other than by his reputation. I don't know him personally in any major way."

"Well that will change once you are married, I am sure that once you get to know him you will probably change your mind about him, he's probably even more interesting when you get to know him personally, instead of just knowing him from afar."

"Well I certainly hope you are right, but I still have my suspicions and my doubts."

"Don't worry, I'm sure that once you are married you will see things differently, just wait and see, in a week all you will be able to talk about is Angry Elk, and you will see him through the eyes that which so many of us have seen him through before. I have to admit though I still am extremely jealous. You are pretty much the one woman in the village who isn't head over heels for him, and yet you are the one who is going to end up marrying him, that hardly seems fair."

I nodded. "I understand, but then maybe it will work out for the best, maybe he needs somebody who isn't going to be head over heels in love with him from the start, maybe that will keep him grounded and make him humble."

Sprinting Rabbit burst out laughing.

"What is so funny?" I demanded.

"The fact that you think that you can tame Angry Elk and make him more humble just shows how not humble you are being right now."

And to that, I had to admit, I had no adequate response.

5

I continued to feel hesitant and apprehensive at the idea of marrying Angry Elk, but for all my protests and doubts and misgivings, I guess I was not willing to defy my father, and I thought to myself that maybe being married to him wouldn't be all that terrible after all, as he was the most eligible hunter and warrior in the entire village, so maybe Sprinting Rabbit was right that it would be a good thing.

It didn't take long for my father and mother and my grandparents to get all excited over the prospect of their granddaughter and their daughter getting married like that.

They arranged the marriage for as soon as possible, and it was going to be a big affair that the entire village would come out to witness.

"I can't believe that my little girl is getting married," my mother said as I dressed in my finest for the occasion. I never really made that big of a deal about clothing, in fact I preferred to spend as much time undressed as possible if I could, and I had to admit that I did look rather good in my wedding get up, even though it had a large number of feathers and I thought that it looked a little bit silly.

"I have to admit I'm still nervous about this whole thing, I mean I have never even been with anybody before, and now I am supposed to move in with somebody that I barely know," I said shaking my head.

"Of course your father and I are going to miss having you around in the house all the time, but it's only natural for children to go off on their own, and it's not like you are going to be far away, we will be in the same village and can see each other every day, you'll just be living a few houses down on the other end of the village where Angry Elk and all of the other warriors like to congregate."

I had to admit that that was another thing that I felt rather apprehensive about, up until now I was used to spending most of my time in the world of women, I wasn't quite sure how I was going to adapt to being the wife of a warrior living in the area of town where all of the warriors tended to go with their wives. It almost felt like I was moving into an entire another world, and in some sense I was, the world of men.

"You look absolutely spectacular, and I feel so happy for you, even if I have never felt more jealous in my entire life," Sprinting Rabbit said as she hugged me. She was all dressed up for the wedding as well, with typical wedding festivities involving people putting lots of feathers on their clothing to symbolize the supposed flight away from my home. Personally I didn't really want to fly away from my home; I just wanted to fly around freely.

I still couldn't help but think that this was going to be the end of my freedom that I had enjoyed up until now. But I am sure that things wouldn't go too fast, it's not like the moment I was married I would be expected to have children the next day, so maybe I was panicking prematurely. I needed to calm down and enjoy myself and just be happy for the arrangement, like everybody told me that I should.

My parents and grandparents escorted me from their house and walked me over to Angry Elk's dwelling at the other end of the village, as everybody in the village came out to cheer, the transition from one home to another, from being the child of my parents to being the wife of my husband.

The village shaman came and did a ceremonial dance as I nervously walked over to the home of my new husband where he was waiting with a big smile on his face. I couldn't help but think that the smile looked almost a little bit lecherous, like the other day at the waterfall. Was that really what he was thinking about on his wedding day?

As the two of us joined hands the village shaman said a bunch of prayers over us and started shaking a rattle at us and putting some paint on our foreheads, symbolizing that we were now one and that we were unified as husband and wife. As soon as that was over everybody in the village started cheering and hooting and hollering, a festive mood over the entire village, which my father said would be good for morale, seeing as it would take away some of the anxiety that people were feeling about the potential for conflict with the other tribes.

Maybe my father was right, if there was going to be a conflict with other tribes at least Angry Elk would be able to protect me. I didn't want to think that I needed protection, but I did not know how to fight or to fend off attackers if our village was attacked, so I would be glad that at least if I was living in the warriors camp I would probably be more well protected there than anywhere else in the village.

We had had a festival not long ago, and I never thought that my next festival would be my own wedding and that it would take place so fast, but before I knew it I was being held up over Angry Elk's head, lifted up like some type of prize trophy as everybody else started cheering and going wild with excitement.

Personally I was relieved when he finally put me down on the ground again. I did want to soar like a bird but not like that!

"Come, we shall dance," Angry Elk said as he took my hand and started dancing with me in the center of the village as everybody danced and sung around us, this being the tradition to celebrate the union of two people in the village.

I know I should have been feeling a lot of pride, being the center of attention like that, but it really was true what I told Sprinting Rabbit, I really didn't like being the center of attention like that, and ever since I started becoming the center of attention I was feeling increasingly self-conscious every time I went out in public. I would actually be rather relieved when all of the festivities were over and I could settle into my new life and start getting used to it.

And although I should be proud of my new husband, his dancing left a lot to be desired, and he kept constantly stepping on my feet and laughing as he did so, as though he were almost taking pleasure in the fact that he was a terrible dancer and that he was hurting my feet, although I didn't want to tell him that and risk wounding his pride or hurting his feelings.

Although I think that the people in the village did have common sense, I think that everybody knew that Angry Elk was not a delicate dancer, there was nothing delicate about him. Everything he did seemed to have to be a display of strength, whether it was lifting me above his head right after being married, or stomping the ground with his feet as though he were trying to stomp down the ground from coming up and attacking him.

I could see his two companions, Howling Wolf and Stalking Badger, standing off to the side clapping continuously and really yukking it up. No matter how terrible a dancer Angry Elk was he could always count on his cronies like that to sing his praises no matter what he did, even if they did it just by clapping on the sidelines like everybody else.

After the ceremonial first dance people started mingling a little bit, and I felt a little bit grateful to not be quite the center of attention that I was earlier. Now I could mingle with my friends and family a little bit.

"So how does it feel to be married?" Sprinting Rabbit asked her eyes wide with wonder, and also with jealousy and excitement.

I shrugged my shoulders. "I guess it feels the same as before I was married, I mean how is it supposed to feel?"

"It should feel like you are dancing on air," she said as she started spinning around and doing a little dance before we both burst out laughing and she pushed me playfully.

"Actually I'm glad to have my feet on the ground at this moment, not being lifted into the air above Angry Elk's head."

"I just can't believe that you are actually married to Angry Elk, I mean I'm always going to be your best friend and everything, but that doesn't mean I can't be as jealous as crazy. And of course there's another reason that I am crazy with jealousy."

"Because you want to be the center of attention?"

She smiled. "Well I certainly wouldn't mind that, but you know what tonight is of course."

"What do you mean what tonight is?"

"Are you really that naïve, it's your wedding night, everybody knows what happens on your wedding night!" As she stared at me in disbelief as though I didn't know what she was talking about. Then she started making motions of throwing her head back and making really contented noises and shouting at which point I got the message and pushed her playfully.

"Shut up," I said, as it was something I really hadn't actually thought about. Were we really expected to immediately get down to business the very first night, wasn't there like a grace period or something?

"You seriously have no idea just how jealous I am of you. He may have gotten to see us already but now you are going to get to see him."

"Well I've already seen most of him," I said, thinking of all of those scars on his body.

"Yeah, but now you're going to see the good stuff,"

she said elbowing me in the side as she burst out laughing. I laughed along with her but I had to admit I was feeling genuinely apprehensive once again now, as I contemplated what was going to happen when we got back to Angry Elk's house once the festivities were over.

"I don't know exactly what I'm supposed to do," I said feeling like an idiot.

She smiled. "Don't worry, I have no doubt that Angry Elk knows exactly what to do, I'm sure he's probably an expert, all you have to do is sit back and enjoy yourself!"

I swallowed deeply, as I was now feeling nervous. I knew that Angry Elk was a big and aggressive guy, and I kind of wondered exactly what it would be like to be with him, in sort of an intimate way. I had not been intimate with anyone like that before, although I had no doubt that for Angry Elk it wouldn't be his first time, not by a long shot, not that I had a problem with that necessarily, as once again I did not really concerned myself with those issues. Although now I was starting to wonder if I should be more concerned with those issues the way everybody else seemed to be.

I took some time off to myself so that I could reflect on the day's events, as I could see it was starting to get closer to evening when we would have the big feast and everything, although I felt butterflies in my stomach and didn't think that I would want to eat all that much.

"So how does it feel to be married," my grandmother said as she came over smiling. "It has been many many moons since my marriage, but I can still remember the day vividly, my first night with your grandfather."

I had to admit my mind immediately went to

perverted thoughts and I started feeling rather awkward about that again.

"Your grandfather carried me across the entire village and was one of the tenderest men that I have ever met," she said, seemingly reminiscing about something that happened long before my birth. "He was a brave warrior but a gentle soul."

"Do you think that Angry Elk will be a gentle soul?" I asked with some degree of nervousness. Angry Elk didn't seem to have that degree of gentleness that my grandfather was known for. He was very rough in every way shape and form, but maybe he was different when he was with women, maybe he was a different person in private behind closed doors, I could only hope so.

My grandmother smiled. "Don't worry young granddaughter, I am sure that whatever happens that you will be happy and that he will treat you right. And someday maybe you'll even be the wife of a chief."

I had to admit that being a prominent individual like that was itself intimidating, but I didn't want to upset my grandmother, so I simply nodded and went along with her over to the dinner table where everybody was gathered for the great feast.

I could see that Angry Elk was already at his privileged place at the head of the table where he was already stuffing his face and drinking heavily. I was kind of hoping that he would be a little bit more well-mannered and graceful on his wedding night, but he seemed to see it as little more than an excuse to eat as much as possible. I was thinking that maybe if he ate enough when we got back to his home maybe he would just want to go right to sleep and I could save my wifely obligations for another time.

As I sat down next to him, as was traditional, I started to eat as well, and the food was actually quite splendid. I felt some degree of guilt as I stuffed my face thinking of all of those people in the neighboring tribes who were suffering from food deprivation, but it was my wedding night, and if you can't indulge yourself on your wedding night when can you?

"Don't eat too much, I don't want to have a fat wife," Angry Elk said as people burst out laughing. I didn't quite find it as funny; did he just insult my weight? Did he say that I was fat? I certainly never considered myself to be fat, in fact I considered myself to be one of the more physically fit women of the tribe.

Angry Elk certainly didn't seem like he was watching his weight, he was probably one of the largest men in the village, and it wasn't all muscle. But as he continued to scarf down his food I felt a little bit more self-conscious as I continued eating mine, and I found that my stomach was starting to feel nervous again, and I found that my appetite was quickly fading.

Finally the day's festivities came to a close and Angry Elk was patting his stomach and looking rather tired. I figured odds were looking pretty good that he would probably just want to go to sleep when we got home. After eating a large meal like that people were often rather exhausted, although I found myself strangely hungry, maybe I should have eaten a little bit more after all. Was I already allowing his insults to get to me?

For a moment I was ready to follow my parents, grandparents and brothers and sisters and go back home with them like I did every day, until I remembered where my new home was.

"Enjoy your first night together," Sprinting Rabbit

said as she winked at me and smiled. I felt like she was looking forward to this night even more than I was, and she was still jealous that she wasn't in my place.

"Come new wife, come see your new home," Angry Elk said as he lifted me up and started carrying me through the entrance of our home before plopping me down on some animal skins on the floor.

As I looked around I saw that it was a sparsely decorated home. I thought that my parents' home was a little bit, I don't know what's the proper word, prettier, with more decorations, but I guess the home of a warrior would probably be less decorative and more practical.

It was a simple home, but it was nothing to complain about, as it looked like it would probably be warm in the winter and cool in the summer. It had dirt floors and a wooden roof and looked like it was adequately built in every way, even if a little bit messy with all sorts of tools and weapons hanging on all corners of the walls.

I looked around and smiled and I didn't want to say anything that would upset him, so I simply nodded. "It's a really nice home; I think that I will sleep well tonight."

As I mentioned that he suddenly went from looking like he was full to suddenly looking like he was hungry again, and by hungry I didn't mean for food. He started looking at me and licking his lips as he put his hands on my chest and started undressing me without even saying so much as a word to me.

Normally I was not bashful, and I know that he had seen me before our wedding night, but as I felt him taking my clothing off from my body I suddenly felt exposed and vulnerable in a way that I never had before, not even on that day in the lake. I instinctively started covering myself up as he started laughing.

I wasn't exactly sure how to respond in a situation like that, so I simply stood there nervously hoping that he would enjoy seeing me like this, even though I was feeling increasingly uncomfortable by the moment. I felt like this was something that everybody else knew how to do just instinctively, and that I was somehow lacking in basic common sense when it came to the arts of intimacy like that. But then maybe it was just experience I lacked, and I was about to get a lesson in that now.

Luckily for me Angry Elk didn't seem to lack for need of instructions, he knew exactly what he was doing, and before I knew it he was done undressing me and pushing me down to the ground and having his way with me. I knew I was supposed to be enjoying this, but something about it was especially savage, he was very rough as he climbed on top of me.

"Do you think you could go a little bit slower, it's hurting me a little bit," I said as he laughed in my face and I could smell the food on his breath. He wasn't gentle the way I was hoping, and he definitely was something of a crude individual.

Blind to my complaints, I decided to just sat back and smile as though I were enjoying it, as I could hear him making all sorts of grunting and groaning noises like he was some type of animal, and he kept going at it until he had finished having his way with me.

As I laid there on the floor, covered in animal skins next to my new husband, I realized that this was our first night together, and I wondered if it was just a preview of what was to come.

I thought that I would sleep well that night, but as Angry Elk started to fall asleep into a gentle slumber I found myself staring at the ceiling and wondering what else the future had in store for me.

6

I found it very difficult to sleep that night in my new home, as it was an unfamiliar environment, and I know that it's often the case where people have a hard time sleeping in a place that they are not familiar with, but I found myself extremely restless just trying to process the events of the day.

In spite of the fact that I didn't sleep very well, unfortunately Angry Elk slept like a baby and was up bright and early in the morning, pushing me to get up when I could have really used the extra sleep after yesterday's festivities.

"Let me sleep a little bit longer," I said tossing around on top of the animal skins as I yawned and rubbed my eyes.

"But you are my wife, it is a wife's duty to make breakfast for her husband," he said as he continued poking me until I eventually waved him off and slowly got up. As I stood up and realized I was still naked I once again felt self-conscious, as the fact that he was looking at me, looking at me smirking, as though I were some type of prize and that I was just another in the latest of his line of conquests.

I was hoping that now that I was his wife hopefully he would be loyal to me and wouldn't be sleeping around with lots of other women, although if he did have other women that would take some of the pressure off of me, as now I felt I was obligated to meet all of his needs, physical, emotional and spiritual, and I wasn't quite exactly sure how to go about that.

As I slowly woke myself up, I began to prepare

breakfast for him. I have to admit that cooking was not one of my greatest skills, but I was hoping that it would be pleasing to my new husband. I cooked some of the fish that he had caught the other day and we still had a lot of food left over from the festivities of yesterday, and I prepared it to the best of my ability and presented it to him.

"What is this," he asked as I placed the food in front of him.

"Well you asked me to make you breakfast, so here we go, I hope you enjoy it."

He looked disagreeably at the food in front of him before looking back at me and giving me a look like I didn't know, like I didn't have the slightest clue what I was doing. But then he began chewing some of it before spitting it out.

"What's the matter was it too hot?" I asked worrying that I had burned his mouth or something like that.

"The flavor isn't exactly right, it has to be cooked just so," he said shaking his head and looking rather disgusted.

"Well I guess I will have to try harder next time and maybe if you tell me how specifically you like it prepared that would help," I said as he sat there with his arms folded as though he were growing impatient.

"Well," he finally said looking at me as though I should automatically know what it was he wanted.

"Well what?"

"You said that you would get it right the next time, so what are you waiting for," he said as he cleared the table of the meal that I had prepared for him and sat there impatiently waiting for me to cook another.

"How do you like it best prepared?"

"I like it prepared in a way that tastes good," he said

with a heavy dose of sarcasm.

I started cooking the next fish, hoping that it would be to his liking, but when I gave it to him another time he still looked at me disagreeably, as though I had failed yet again.

"What's the matter, what did I do wrong this time?" I eventually asked him.

He frowned at me as though I had been asking him a rhetorical question of some kind, before he continued eating while looking up at me and shaking his head.

I knew that I wasn't the best chef in the world but I was hoping that something as simple as cooking fish for breakfast would be pleasing to him, but apparently it wasn't. Already I was failing at being a dutiful wife to him and I couldn't help wonder how I would disappoint him next.

When he had finished his breakfast and I had finished mine I began cleaning up when all of a sudden he grabbed me by the arm.

"What is it, what do you want," I said as he looked at me with that same lecherous smile that he did the other night as he licked his lips and nodded his head.

"Again, but we just did it last night," I said wondering how often it was that married couples tended to get down to business, so to speak.

"I like it frequently," he said as he laughed.

I had to admit I was still feeling kind of dirty from everything that had happened last night, I was always told that something like this was supposed to be mutually pleasurable and it was the greatest experience of life, but I have to say that he left me sorely lacking and disappointed, but I didn't want to disappoint him.

He stood there tapping his foot impatiently as I

slowly started getting undressed and a smile appeared across his face as I complied with his wishes. I could see that he was enjoying every moment of this, and it made me wonder how many times he had been looking at me in the past with a similar eye without me ever really noticing that he was paying me such attention. Maybe I really was naïve and oblivious to the ways of the world, and in particular to the ways of men, men and more specifically warriors like Angry Elk.

"Dance around a little bit for me," he said smiling, as I began doing a dance causing certain parts of my anatomy to jiggle about in a way that he seemed to find pleasing. When I stopped he began clapping. "More, do it some more."

I had to admit, as I stood there dancing naked in front of him, I was feeling rather ridiculous with the whole situation. Is this really what it was like to be part of a married couple? Is this how married couples tended to start their day every morning? As far as I knew my parents and grandparents didn't do this every morning, but then maybe things change once you have children.

Finally when I was done dancing around to his satisfaction he came over to me as he began undressing, before pushing me to the ground again and having his way with me. I was hoping this time he would be less rough and perhaps he would display a little bit more gentleness, but this time he seemed like he was actually rougher than the first time, even cruder, but luckily this time it didn't last as long before he smiled with that look of satisfaction on his face.

I was wondering if this was going to be how it was like every time, did you always feel sort of gross and dirty after the act? I was starting to wonder why people had sung its praises so much, as I was finding myself less than impressed. However I simply smiled at him as though I had enjoyed the entire affair, even though my enjoyment didn't seem to really be of concern to him, except insofar as it tended to bolster his ego as a man.

"I feel like I want to go to the lake and wash off," I said hoping to get the dirty feeling off of my body. I had never felt dirty like this before, but I felt it was an unpleasant feeling, and that I wanted to get it off of me as soon as possible.

He shook his head. "It's not safe for women to go out alone."

"I can take care of myself, I don't need you to escort me everywhere I go," I said, even though I realized that that was just the advice that was agreed upon by my father as well. I knew that he was just worrying about my well-being, or at least he seemed to be, but I didn't feel like being led around like I was an infant when I had gone to the lake by myself or with Sprinting Rabbit all the time.

He shook his head again. "I forbid you from going out of this house without me to accompany you, and today I have important hunting that I have to do, as well as scouting the area for potential enemies. I'm afraid that you will just have to stay here by yourself."

"You want me to stay here all day by myself, what am I supposed to do by myself all day?"

"Clean up the house, and learn better cooking skills, your breakfast left much to be desired," he said and for a moment I felt infuriated and wanted to slap him, but given that he could hit me back a lot harder I knew that it would be a foolish idea, so I simply nodded my head and complied.

As he began to get his weapons to go out with his

hunting party I felt a little bit relieved that he was going to be gone for the day and give me some time to myself, where I wouldn't be under his constant scrutiny or bellowing of demands.

"When do you think you will be back?" I asked as he prepared to leave with his two sniveling sycophantic companions, who as usual weren't saying anything to contradict anything that he said and were just nodding with him in agreement at everything that he did say.

"Why, are you hoping to sneak out on me, perhaps with other men," he said looking at me with suspicion.

"No, I just wanted to know when you were going to be home, you know so I can have dinner and everything ready on time," I said, figuring that that's what he would like to hear.

He shook his head. "I'll be home when I get home, and when I get home you had better be here. I will not tolerate my wife going around and fraternizing with other men behind my back."

We weren't even married a full day yet and already he was looking at me as a potential adulterer who was cheating on him. This was especially frustrating, seeing as I knew that he was likely not to be as monogamous in this couple as I was expected to be, although I was hoping that maybe if I didn't anger him he would eventually start to treat me more gingerly and would be faithful to me.

Angry Elk and his companions set out to go on their hunt, but I found it personally insulting that he didn't trust me to be faithful to him for a couple of hours while he was out with his friends. I got around to cleaning the house and tried my best to learn a better way to prepare dinner, but I didn't know exactly if the way I was preparing it would be pleasing to him.

I didn't want to believe that being married would be a major restriction on my freedom, but it seemed like it already was. Already my husband was forbidding me to leave the house without him, as though if I left the house without him I would immediately be going to see other men. That was a ridiculous notion, and if he realized that last night was the first time I had ever been with a man he would probably not believe it.

That I started thinking to myself that maybe I had done something wrong. Maybe if I had been better when we were intimate he wouldn't be going off to seek other companions or be distrustful of me. Perhaps I should have been feeling a sense of pride; after all he was the first man who ever treated me as a woman with a woman's body, who was looking at me with the eyes of an adult as an adult woman.

During the course of the day Sprinting Rabbit came around to see how I was doing.

"How's the luckiest lady in the world today," she said as she peeked around the doorway I said as I ran over and hugged her. "So how is married life treating you so far, was Angry Elk everything that you were expecting?"

I once again shrugged my shoulders. "I think what you are really asking is was he everything that *you* were expecting."

"Well that is certainly true," she said, with me not exactly sure how to answer her question. "I mean maybe it's none of my business and everything like that, but please tell me all about it!"

I could see that she was very excited over the prospect that I had slept with Angry Elk, but based on my experience I didn't understand why she was so excited about the prospect, but I didn't want to say anything that could end up leading to gossip about Angry Elk that would wound his pride or hurt his masculine feelings as a man.

"It was interesting, it was different," I said stumbling for the correct words to use to describe it. I wasn't very good at describing an experience like this, and I think that she was expecting me to describe it as the most wonderful thing in the world, where as for me I thought that it was somewhat unpleasant in all honesty.

"Interesting and different from what, he was the first man you have ever been with, wasn't he?"

I nodded.

"So what was he like, you know behind closed doors, intimately and everything," she said with a perverted little smile on her face. "I know you don't have anything to compare it to, but it must have been quite the experience!"

"Well it was a little bit rough I guess, it kind of hurt a little bit," I said being fully honest.

She nodded. "Don't worry, you'll get used to it, I've heard that it hurts a bit the first time."

"Well it hurt a lot the second time as well," I said shaking my head before realizing what I had said as I saw her eyes light up.

"You've already done it two times since last night, are you trying to make me die of jealousy right now?"

"How is it supposed to feel?"

"It's supposed to feel like the most wonderful thing in the world, like you are literally walking on air."

"I wasn't so much walking on air, as I was on the floor really."

"So is he a real animal in bed?" her enthusiasm being misplaced as far as I was concerned.

"I guess you could say that he was like an animal, he

always seems like he is on the hunt."

At that moment I realized perhaps that wasn't the most flattering thing to say, it made it sound like he was the one hunting me and that I was the prey, but we were husband and wife, we were supposed to be equal partners, not a predator and the object of their query.

"I know, that's what's so dreamy about him," she said as her eyes started lighting up again. I could tell she was already fantasizing about my husband, and if I were a different type of woman that would be making me the one jealous, but I guess seeing as it was her and I knew that she didn't mean anything by it, well I guess there was no cause for me to get angry, I just quite didn't understand the way she was seeing things.

I was about to say more when Angry Elk and his companions came back with what looked like a deer over his shoulders, a nice juicy one, an even bigger one than the one that we saw the other day.

"Hi Angry Elk," Sprinting Rabbit said, looking as though she were completely giddy. It was weird seeing a woman head over heels in love with your husband, let alone your best friend, when you didn't quite understand what she saw in him the same way that she apparently did.

"What are you doing with guests over," Angry Elk said as he put down the catch of the day. "I told you that you shouldn't leave the house today."

"But I didn't leave anywhere, she came to see me, you didn't say I couldn't have anybody else over," I said. "Besides you know her, she's my best friend."

He nodded. "Yes I know her," he said in sort of a dismissive way that caused her to frown, suggesting that he didn't really ever take much notice of her, which was a blow to her own ego, which while not as big as his, was not exactly small either.

"I figured that maybe she could stay for dinner and everything like that," I finally said, realizing that we had a good catch of the day.

"A husband and wife should eat dinner together, as an intimate thing," he said giving Sprinting Rabbit an intimidating stare down as though he did not approve of me talking to her, even though he said that he only didn't want any men coming over or me going to see any men, having said nothing about other women, who surely shouldn't cause him such jealousy.

"It's okay, I have food at home, and I guess I should probably be going anyway," Sprinting Rabbit said, feeling as though she had been given her walking papers and looking more than a little bit disappointed.

I wanted to tell her not to go, and felt bad she was being made to feel unwelcome, but I could see that Angry Elk didn't want her there, and I could see that his companions were getting ready to leave as well, so once again I was with him alone. I would have loved to have gone down to the lake with Sprinting Rabbit, but now I was kind of glad that I didn't bring up the suggestion, because if I hadn't been home when he arrived he probably would have been quite angry.

Once everybody had left I started preparing some of the deer for us to eat for dinner that night. It looked especially succulent, and I was hoping that I would do a better job of cooking it to his satisfaction than I did the fish. This would provide us with food for quite a while, but just the same I didn't want to risk wasting any of it, especially when I knew that people in other villages nearby were starving and weren't eating quite as well as I was. In that regard I guess I should be thankful for Angry Elk, he really was a good provider as far as being a hunter goes.

Fortunately it seemed like he enjoyed the deer more than he did the fish, although occasionally he gave me a grimace as though he didn't fully approve of it fully. I wanted to ask him what was wrong but I figured as long as I didn't say anything he wouldn't bring it up.

"So how was your day hunting," I eventually asked him.

He looked at me as though I was silly and laughed.

"What exactly is so funny?" I asked.

"Well you can see that I had a good hunting day, is this not enough food for you, how much weight do you want to gain anyway?" he said as he began laughing rather loudly.

I was not appreciating his comments on my weight, especially since I was well known to be slender. But I guess he was afraid that there was even the remote possibility of me getting fat, and he probably figured having a fat wife would reflect negative on him, especially seeing as the more I was eating the more he looked at me as though I were some type of a filthy animal.

When we had finished our dinner I figured he was probably going to want to go right to sleep after hunting all day and probably being tired, he certainly worked up an appetite at any rate. But it looked like hunting worked up an appetite for something other than just food, and as soon as I was done cleaning up after dinner I already found him grabbing me and pulling my clothes off of my body and throwing me down on the floor.

It hurt the third time as well.

7

I soon found myself falling into a regular routine with

Angry Elk, as much as I didn't want to find myself in that particular situation. Every morning I would make him breakfast and he would usually give me a disapproving glance, as it was not to his specifications or was not up to his standards. I would often try many times to cook it to his satisfaction, but he continued to send it back before reluctantly eating it, usually while grimacing in disapproval the whole time. Then when I would try eating he would complain that I was eating too much and say that I was going to get fat if I kept up like that, even though I didn't really consider myself to eat all that much as well.

In fact as far as eating went I found myself eating a lot less since I was married. A lot of people say that they start eating more when they are married because they are no longer trying to attract a mate, but I found that the opposite was the case for me, I felt guilty every time I was eating when he was looking at me, as though it were some type of unforgivable act simply to feed myself. And I would say that he ate at least two or three times as much as I did, and even some of my friends commented that it looked like I was losing noticeable amounts of weight.

Angry Elk's sexual needs were much more extensive, where he would always want to go before bed and then again in the morning, and then often he would come home in the middle of the day demanding more sex, and it was always rough and unpleasant, with me being just like a prop for his own personal pleasure. The only good thing I can say was that it was usually quick, as it didn't take long for him to satisfy his carnal urges.

Fortunately he spent most of the day away hunting and scavenging the land. He expected me to stay home during most of the day, which I found to be rather boring and confining, him using the excuse that there could be danger out there from enemy tribes.

Once in a while he would let me go gathering food in the forest but he would usually ask that he come with me, where I would gather food while he and his companions would hunt for food. And no matter what I gathered he would always look at it as though it were some type of lesser contribution compared to his hunting.

In fairness the bulk of our diet consisted of what he managed to hunt, whereas what I managed to gather tended to be more like the appetizer or the window-dressing of our meals, but he would always diminish my accomplishments, especially in front of his two sycophantic companions, who would continue to laugh and nodded in agreement every time he happened to insult me or to put me down in some way, or to minimize my contributions.

Often while I was gathering food I could hear him talking to his friends about what a great lover he was and how much sex he was getting from me, as though I were begging him for it. It was rather interesting that when he talked about me to his friends he never mentioned that he thought that I was fat or unattractive, only when it was just he and I alone.

Occasionally I would feel like contradicting him in front of his friends, I felt like going up to them and saying that he was a terrible lover and wounding his pride like that, but I knew better and held my tongue because I didn't know how he would react. The last thing I wanted to do was make him angry, because when he was angry he was an even more aggressive lover and me even more irritable to be around.

This routine continued for several weeks and soon it just became a normal pattern. Every morning breakfast, sex, housework, occasional food gathering, always under his watchful eye, then time to prepare his meal for dinner and then more sex followed by a restless and uncomfortable sleep.

I found myself feeling frequently dirty from all of the sweaty lovemaking that he subjected me to, and only occasionally did he let me go down to the lake to wash off, and every time I would do so he would watch me. I hadn't been to the lake with Sprinting Rabbit with just the two of us like we had been in weeks. She would come by to visit every so often, but I had the feeling that Angry Elk made her feel unwelcome, and soon I found myself increasingly lonely and isolated, as though I were a prisoner of his home.

My parents and grandparents said that he was just rough around the edges, and that over time he would probably start to become more accommodating to me, I just had to work my charms on him. Maybe I just had a deficit of charms, but whatever I was doing didn't seem to be working. As the weeks went on I found him just as irritable and horny and crude as he was in the beginning, perhaps even more so.

Although I satisfied his sexual urges whenever he demanded of me, I had no doubt that while he was out hunting he was probably also hunting for other women. Although he would scowl at me if he ever saw me talking to a man who wasn't a blood relative, I found him regularly talking to women in the village, often in a boastful manner, sometimes flexing his muscles and pointing to his many battle scars as a way of showing off, despite the fact that everybody knew he was now a married man.

Personally I didn't care all that much about his infidelity, seeing as if others were satisfying him it meant that I would have less to satisfy him with later. If he came home exhausted from one of his affairs I knew that at least I would be spared his advances for the night and could hopefully get a better sleep, without that dirty and exhausted feeling that always came after our bouts of lovemaking.

As he kept me from my friends and family more and more, I began to resent him, in fact as I saw him grimacing whenever he would eat my cooking I felt almost good, almost feeling like I was getting some subtle revenge on him by assaulting his taste buds. It was hard not to smile at him when I saw him frown. If I were a lesser woman I might even try poisoning him to make him less aggressive just so I would be spared his constant attention and scrutiny.

However in this marriage I realized that I had to be the bigger person if I was to survive. And that's the way it started to feel over time, it felt like not just I was enduring him, but I was trying to survive him. I kept telling myself that over time maybe he would improve, or that maybe when the threat to the village wasn't quite as high maybe I could find some way to break away from him, even though it would be a big scandal and a disgrace.

As much as my increasingly infrequent visits from my family members who came to reassure me that things would get better with time, I was starting to realize that that was not the case, and soon it was becoming almost intolerable to be spending any amount of time with Angry Elk.

On the even more infrequent opportunities I had to spend time with Sprinting Rabbit she would ask how things were going, and I would complain and she would look at me as though she didn't quite believe me, with that same look of jealousy, like I didn't know how good I had it by being married to Angry Elk.

Personally I never knew exactly what she saw in him that was so great. Maybe physically he wasn't that unattractive or anything like that, but there were certainly better men in the village than he. I couldn't help but feel that maybe Sprinting Rabbit simply resented the fact that I was now a married woman, and maybe she falsely got the impression that I thought I was somehow superior to her, which wasn't the case at all. Believe me if she asked if we could trade I would give him a way to her in a second, except I wouldn't want her to be subjected to his constant attention either, because then she would realize how far from pleasant he was behind closed doors.

The most frustrating thing about all of it was that few people seemed to believe me whenever I said anything bad about him. That was something I never fully understood, it wasn't just Sprinting Rabbit who was making excuses for him, it seemed like everyone was saying that maybe I was just spoiled by being a pampered housewife or wasn't accustomed to the new responsibilities of marriage, but if anybody was spoiled it was certainly Angry Elk, who was treating me more like a sexual object or a servant there to fulfill and gratify his every need and urge rather than some type of equal partner.

I guess that the people in the village only saw the face that he presented to the world, as the boastful and strong hunter who was providing so much food for the village, but all the while I was going to sleep hungry because I didn't want to eat too much in front of him, lest he complained about my growing weight, when in fact everybody noticed that I was losing weight, and yet still did not believe the bad things I would say about him, saying that I just had to get used to marriage and that I was the luckiest woman in the village.

Personally I felt that almost every other woman in the village was luckier than I was, any one of them would have made a better companion for Angry Elk and vice versa. I was trying to think of some way I could perhaps get out of the marriage, even if it ended up being a scandal. I just knew that I didn't want to live like this for the rest of my life, and I didn't know how much longer I could take it.

However that all changed one day when Howling Wolf and Stalking Badger burst in through the door of the home carrying Angry Elk on their shoulders with the blood coming down his leg and what looked like an injury on his arm as well.

"By the great spirit, what has happened," I said as I saw the wound on his arms and legs, only distinguishable from his other scars because they were fresh and still bleeding.

"We encountered members of an enemy tribe who caught us without warning, luckily we were able to drive them off but not before they injured him," Stalking Badger said.

"Here let me get something for the wound," I said as I started making some bandages for him and putting some medicine on the bandages as I slowly applied it to the wound causing him to scream. "Sorry it may sting a little bit, but this is going to help you to get better."

"We should probably go and tell members of the village council that we came under attack today," Howling Wolf said as they prepared to leave.

"Wait, what am I supposed to do?" I said, not sure how to handle this situation.

"You know how to treat a wound, he is your

husband you must take care of him," Stalking Badger said as he left me once again alone with Angry Elk.

Although for a moment I felt sympathetic to his condition and felt bad about all of the complaints I had made about him, as soon as he hit me across the face for aggravating his wound when I started to wrap his arm up, I knew that it was going to be a difficult couple of days, and that a man who had already been very irritable was most likely going to get a lot more irritable.

I was not looking forward to it.

8

I had been telling myself that there was nothing worse than living with Angry Elk, but there was something worse than living with him, there was living with him when he was injured and was even more irritable than he was before, more crude, but no less carnal and no less demanding.

I was hoping the fact that he was injured and incapacitated would perhaps make him more docile, but I found that the opposite was the case. Now I was stuck at home with him pretty much all the time. At least during the day when he was out with his fellow warriors and hunters I had the day to myself. Although I was lonely I was used to being alone, as I didn't need constant companionship, let alone companionship that I found disagreeable, such as his company.

"I'm hungry, get me some food," he would frequently bellow first thing in the morning. I would then prepare his breakfast for him and he would look at it in a similar disagreeable manner, sometimes throwing it right back in my face. I tried to tell myself that he was just angry because he was in pain, and even if that was in the case though it didn't excuse the fact that his behavior was increasingly cruel and abusive.

Every day I would check his wounds, and every day as I applied the medicine to it he would scream out loud and often end up hitting me in the process. Again I tried to look the other way on this matter, seeing as I knew he was in pain, but considering that he was such a brave and strong warrior you would think that he would be able to tolerate a little pain like that without being such a baby about it.

But every couple of minutes he had a new demand of me. He would want me to get him something, he would want me to make him something, or he would want me to pleasure him in some way. Seeing as he was not up to the aggressive and rough sex that he was accustomed to, he frequently had me pleasure him in other ways, such as with my hands or my mouth, and that seemed to please him, as much as it displeased me.

Every time I even dared to complain he would say that he got injured fighting protecting the village and that he was a great warrior and that I should be so lucky to be married to such a wonderful human being. However every day that I spent with him, now uninterrupted with hardly a minute's peace, he was proving less and less what a wonderful human being he was with each passing moment.

I was hoping that as his wounds began to heal that maybe he would become less irritable and he would start hunting again, but unfortunately his wounds were rather severe, and he would have to stay off of his leg for a while. Raiding parties attacking from the enemy villages started becoming more frequent and that left us fewer opportunities to go out into the forest without having supervision.

"No, I forbid you from going out," he would say

with his arms folded and looking at me like I was as promiscuous in his mind as he was in actuality.

I would try to argue with him that if he wanted me to get more food and supplies, seeing as now we were relying on charity from other hunters, gatherers and fishers, that I would have to leave the house, but he insisted that people came here and delivered it to him directly. If he couldn't leave the house, his reasoning was going, then I couldn't leave the house either.

Once again, although I did not particularly care whether he was faithful to me one way or another, he cared very much that I was faithful to him, and the fact that he seemed to think that every time I wanted to leave the house that it was to be with other men I found personally insulting. Personally if any other men in the world where anything like him I would be done with men for good and all for all I cared.

Each day Howling Wolf and Stalking Badger would come with food for me to prepare, and often they would stay for a while, but then they would leave, not wanting to endure an irritable Angry Elk any more than I wanted to. I wouldn't have minded having them around longer, because at least then if they were spending time with him that would be less attention that was focused on me.

However when they were there I was at the constant mercy of his verbal abuse. No matter how tender I treated him, no matter how much I gave into his demands, he never seemed to be satisfied in the least bit. He would complain endlessly to his friends about how pleasing he was and how ungrateful I was for being married to the most eligible man in the village.

My sympathy for his injuries started diminishing over time, and I didn't just not love him, but I found myself actively resenting him, even hating him. Every moment I spent with him was a moment that was making me more enraged, making me just wish that I could get out of there, that I could leave him and never have to pay him attention ever again.

In fact as the days went on and Angry Elk became even more intolerable, as he couldn't stop scratching at his wounds and throwing stuff at me, I considered more and more the possibility of simply abandoning him. Then I would always end up feeling guilty, to abandon an injured warrior like that and leave him to his own devices, however abusive he might be, just didn't seem like the right thing to do.

Each night after having to fulfill all of his desires, physical mental and emotional, and above all sexual, I would say a silent prayer to the great spirit that hopefully he would recover soon and that he would become a more tolerable person, although sometimes in anger I found myself praying that he would die and that I would be free of him forever. But then I would feel guilty and pray for forgiveness for my hateful thoughts towards him.

As his abuse continued however, the hateful thoughts became more and more frequent, until practically all I could think about was just how life would be much better without him. Every time he laid his hands on me, every time he yelled at me, every time he made a demand, I felt that my anger was reaching closer and closer to its limit. I would talk back to him occasionally, but that would just make him more aggressive, and then I would become frightened of him. Even injured and semi-incapacitated he was an intimidating man to be around, and he was not used to being told no whenever he demanded anything.

Everything came to a head one night while we were

sitting in front of the fire and attempting to keep warm on a particularly cold night. As we sat around the fire saying little I couldn't help but notice that he was looking at me, looking at me as though I were some filthy disgusting creature.

"What's the matter," I finally asked.

"You're seeing other men aren't you," he eventually said.

"Seeing other men, what are you talking about, I am here with you all day long, when would I even have the chance to see other men?"

"You wait for me to go to sleep and then you go and cavort with other men, you are a filthy and disloyal woman."

"But I do no such thing!" I said finding myself increasingly frustrated with his constant abuse and accusations, unfounded accusations at that. "And the only time I feel filthy is after being with you. I sit around waiting on you hand and foot and fulfilling your every need, of which there are many, but do you once ever fulfill my needs?"

"You are obviously not going hungry," he said pointing to his stomach and moving his hands out expanding it as though he will once again saying that I were fat.

"I am not fat!" I said as I pointed to my stomach. "I weigh a heck of a lot less than you do, and I eat a whole lot less than you do. You eat so much I don't even know how it all fits in your stomach."

"But I am a warrior; I need my food to be strong and healthy, and to protect weak people like you."

"I am not weak!"

The two of us stood there staring at each other, and

although I didn't want to lose face and wanted to stand my ground, he gave me that intimidating glare that I realized is the same glare that he gave everybody else that made them feel diminished, that made them feel afraid. And even though he was currently injured, I still felt intimidated by him, and as much as I was beginning to hate him, in that moment he looked so pathetic that I found myself having a perverse sympathy for him in spite of everything.

We didn't say anything for several minutes until he started to smile. "Why don't you do a little dance for me in front of the fire?"

I began to dance in front of the fire but he shook his head and indicated that I should undress. I was reluctant to do so, but I figured if I satisfied his need for this maybe that would be enough for tonight, maybe then he would go to sleep and be quiet and I could get some peace and quiet for myself.

I slowly undressed as he stood there staring at me, watching my shadow dance naked on the walls of the house reflecting around the fire. He began clapping and smiling as I did a little dance for him and he indicated that I should bring my clothing over to him.

I reluctantly handed him my clothing, as he went over to the animal skins and sat on top of them.

"What are you doing?" I asked, finding his behavior most peculiar.

"I don't know if you have noticed but I have hidden most of the rest of your clothing, and now that I have your last piece of clothing I know that you will probably stay here and will not go out to seek other lovers in the night," he said with a lecherous smile. He seemed like he was getting a power rush on the fact that he had possession of my clothing.

I didn't know exactly what to say until I realized that it was true, I didn't know what he had done with the rest of my clothing, or even that he took my clothing until that moment, and now the only piece of clothing that I had was currently in his possession and I was standing there naked and feeling like a fool.

"But now come on, come to bed with me," he said patting the animal skins. As much as I didn't want to get anywhere near him at the moment, I realized that it was best that I try to appease him. Maybe in the morning he would come to his senses and stop playing all of these silly games.

I got on top of the animal skins with him and he pulled me close, and I could smell the food on his breath. He moved my hands down to his genitals and indicated that I should please him with my hands, and I reluctantly did so as a relaxed look came over his face and he slowly started to fall asleep.

Once I was sure he was asleep I slowly got up and moved away from the animal skins. I looked at my clothing firmly under his body and I knew that there was no way I could get it back without waking him. At that moment though I realized that I had had enough, that after everything that we had been through together, this was the final straw and I couldn't stand another night with him.

Slowly and quietly I walked across the room and I picked up his hunting knife. It looked good and sharp and I found myself very slowly approaching his sleeping body. I thought that maybe if I did it quickly it would all be over. I would just tiptoe over to him and before he even knew what hit him I would stuff the knife into his throat and I would be free of him forever.

If I did it the right way it could even look like a

nocturnal raid by one of the enemy tribes. That would be a believable story, as nobody would believe that somebody like me was able to overpower someone like him and kill him. I could wake up in the morning screaming about how somebody had killed my husband and put on a really good show of it.

That wasn't such a terrible plan under the circumstances, I would finally rid myself of my one biggest problem in the world and nobody would even think to blame me. They would think that he had been killed in the middle of the night by an enemy tribe and that I was a poor widow.

Then I thought though if they killed him why wouldn't they kill me as well? Maybe the plan wasn't exactly flawless, and I soon found myself losing my nerve. As I looked at him sleeping and snoring I held the knife tightly in my hand. I also thought to myself that if I stabbed him once and he managed to wake up would he still be able to overpower me?

Even though he was injured and vulnerable, I figured if I got close enough to stab him he might wake up and be able to grab me and make short work of me. I may not have been a defenseless and delicate little creature the way he thought I was, but I still wasn't the biggest and most formidable hunter and warrior in the entire village the way he was either. And he almost seemed like he was larger-than-life, like he was the size of a house.

As I stood over his body holding the knife over it I found my hand trembling and my resolve diminishing. No, I was not a murderer, I could not kill Angry Elk, no matter how angry I was at him, and no matter how much I hated him. It just wasn't in my nature to kill a man, even a terrible man, even a man that I felt was a potential threat to me.

As I lowered the knife to my side however, and continued staring at him on top of my clothing, I knew that things could not continue like this indefinitely. Something had to give and it had to be me.

I thought I should look around for the rest of my clothing, as he probably couldn't have hidden it anyplace too far away, but if he caught me outside of the house who knows what he would do to me? I wasn't sure if he would be able to give chase with his injuries still causing him pain, but I wasn't about to take that risk.

So, with the knife by my side I walked out into the cold night air and walked away from Angry Elk forever. I was alone, I was cold and I was naked, but I never felt better, because once again I was finally free and standing on my own 2 feet.

9

I stood there feeling the cold night air against my naked flesh giving me goosebumps and for a moment I felt inclined to turn back. Was I really willing to turn my back when everything that I knew? I had a lot more than my husband to consider, as I had friends and family in the village, but I felt as long as Angry Elk was alive and respected in the village that I would never be accepted, I would be seen as that woman who wanted to abandon her husband after he was injured in combat. Forget the fact that they didn't know what was going on behind closed doors, didn't see his true nature on display, I realized that I would probably never be believed.

For a long time I stood outside of my home, a place that had only been my home for a short time, but that had mostly bad memories associated with it, as I thought of the positive memories I had with my greater village in contrast to my bad experiences in my husband's home. I briefly considered the possibility that going back to him might be something I could endure for a little while longer, maybe bide my time a little bit, instead of just running off into night never to return.

I then began hearing the bellowing of Angry Elk from inside the house shouting for me and wondering where I had gone, no doubt assuming that I had probably gone off to see other men. As I heard him yelling and screaming for me that was when my mind was firmly made up, there was no going back, no way, no how, never.

I took one last look at the village that had been my home for so long, shook my head and started running off deep into the forest at night.

I had not spent a lot of time in the woods at night; I was more accustomed to what it looked like during the day. In the night there were all sorts of sounds of animals and other creatures that you didn't hear of during the day. That alone started to make me start feeling intimidated once again, thinking that maybe I had made the wrong decision, but maybe I couldn't cut it by myself living out in the middle of nowhere, naked and cold and alone.

But if I wanted to be a free woman again I knew this was the only way to go. I could only hope that I wouldn't encounter enemies from another tribe, or if I did maybe they would take me in and make me part of their tribe, not that I really wanted to be part of another tribe.

I knew that I had to find someplace warm for the night so that I wouldn't freeze, so I quickly gathered up a bunch of wood and made my way to a cave that I knew nearby that would hopefully provide a home for me where I could stay warm for the night.

I started a fire at the mouth of the cave, both to keep me warm and to keep anything outside of the cave from coming in. As I stood there around the fire warming my cold body I started to feel better again, I started to feel firmer in my resolve that I had done the right thing.

"I may not be a champion hunter and warrior like Angry Elk, but I can take care of myself, I am not a helpless infant," I said as I looked at my reflection on the cave wall, a reflection that looked a lot larger than I actually was, but for a moment it made me feel big, made me feel like a larger and more powerful person than I actually was.

I eventually sat down around the fire and waited until I had gotten warm enough that I felt I could sleep. It took me a long time to fall asleep, as I thought of how my husband would respond when he found that I had gone missing. No doubt he would assume that I was off with another man, something that would wound his pride, and after the way he had treated me I felt good about that, I wanted him to feel bad about me disappearing, wanted him to realize how much I did for him so that he would appreciate me more now that I was gone.

I'll admit I went to sleep that night feeling smug at my stand against him, feeling that now he would see how difficult it was to be left alone like that. For a moment I felt guilty about that, but my guilt started diminishing with each passing moment as I thought about how badly he treated me. The fact that I walked away from him without trying to do him any greater harm showed that I was the bigger person, and that I was just looking out for my own safety and well-being. I had no doubt that if I stayed with him things would've only gotten worse, he would have gotten more abusive, and who knows what could happen in the long run, whether he would even tolerate me alive.

When I woke up the next morning I was feeling a lot warmer, even though the fire had extinguished itself. Considering I slept naked in a cave I actually felt rather rested and relaxed, in fact considering that I was now free again I felt almost exhilarated, euphoric even.

As I walked out of the cave into the morning sunlight and looked at the environment around me I couldn't help but think that Angry Elk was probably just waking up bellowing for sex and demanding that I make him breakfast, only to realize that he wouldn't be getting either this morning. I laughed to myself as I thought of him waking up to an empty bed with nobody there to help him, making him realize how helpless and how infantile he was, just a big baby at heart when it came down to it.

As I thought of him not getting any breakfast it occurred to me that I had to find some breakfast of my own, so I wasted no time in looking through the forest for something to eat. I found a bunch of acorns and berries and other things around the forest that at least would tide me over. In the long run I would have to learn to hunt and fish for myself, although I didn't think that that was much of a problem, as I knew the basics.

I walked around the forest and I briefly paused as I heard more people coming, people that I didn't recognize. This is exactly what I had worried about, people from another tribe. What would they do if they found me? Would they rape me or kill me?

I certainly didn't intend to find out, so I made sure to hide myself and watched until they left. That reminded me that it was still really dangerous out there and I was not very well protected. I had taken Angry Elk's knife with me, so I had some form of protection, but in the long run I would have to find someplace safe that I could go, someplace where I wouldn't have to worry about being raped or killed by members of an enemy tribe.

I had gone rogue and now I was sort of a renegade, I had no tribe to call my own anymore; I had left my own tribe and was now out on my own. For a moment I felt like it would be a lonely existence, but then I felt for the first time in my life I was really and truly free, free from the expectations of others, free from obligations to others, and free from the judgment of others.

I didn't quite care what people would think of me having abandoned my husband like that, as I never saw him as a husband to me, more of an infiltrator, someone who had taken my life from me, and now I had taken it back. For the first time ever in my life I felt really and truly my own, I felt powerful, and it was not a feeling that I wanted to give up.

"No, there will be no running back for me," I said becoming more firm in my resolve to get as far from here as possible.

Feeling rather dirty still, I decided to make my way to the lake to wash myself off. It was good to be able to go to the lake unaccompanied by Angry Elk, but it made me sad briefly as I thought about all of the good times I had had there with Sprinting Rabbit. I would miss her and I would give anything just to hear her voice one last time.

"Singing Waterfall," I heard her say as I turned around to face her. It seems like my prayers had been answered.

"Sprinting Rabbit!" I said as I hugged her. "You have no idea how good it is to see you. What are you doing down here?"

"I guess thought I would go for a dip in the lake, I

haven't washed myself in a while and everything. What are you doing here without Angry Elk?"

"I don't need his permission to do everything," I said, lying and not wanting to tell her that I had abandoned him. I could see that there was a look of suspicion in her eye but I didn't really feel like confessing to what I had done, or what I was planning to do. For now I just wanted to enjoy one last moment with a good friend of mine, so at that moment I began splashing her.

Soon it was just like old times, we were splashing each other in the lake and having a grand old time, and for a moment it almost made me want to go back to the village, swallow my pride and try to make the best of a bad situation. But then I thought that after this Angry Elk would never forgive me. If the price of living in this village was having to live with him it was a price that was too high for me to pay.

When it was all over, and she was getting dressed and getting ready to go back to the village, she looked at me and gave me an odd look.

"Where are your clothes?" she finally asked.

I could tell that she knew something was suspicious, and I figured that I had to come clean, although I didn't want to tell her about the fact that I wouldn't be coming back, I felt it would be easier that way, so I decided to try to think of the best way to break things to her.

"Sprinting Rabbit, you have been a good friend to me, but I am afraid that I will be have to be going away for a while."

She gave me a puzzled look. "What do you mean going away, going away where?"

"I can't explain, I just I have to get away for a little while."

"For how long, where will you go? What about Angry Elk?"

"I just need some time to myself, some time to be alone; do you understand what I am saying?"

As the two of us looked at each other and she stood there watching me stand there naked with that forlorn look on my face, with that wandering eye looking towards the horizon, I felt that somehow she understood, she didn't need to say it, but she knew that something had changed.

"But you'll be back right?" she eventually asked.

I didn't want to lie to her, but the truth was too harsh, and I think that she knew I was lying when I nodded my head. "Don't worry I'll be back, but until then take care of yourself, okay?"

"You too," she said as the two of us hugged as she reluctantly turned to me and started to walk back to the village. I continued watching her until she had disappeared from view, then slowly turning around and facing the unknown world in front of me I started taking my next steps and following the river, not sure exactly where it was going to take me, but I knew it was going to take me away from here, and I knew that I wouldn't be coming back anytime soon, if ever.

10

I followed the river, walking for several days. Using Angry Elk's knife I managed to find a large stick that I managed to sharpen into a spear, and I was able to use that to spear fish that I was then able to cook. That along with what I managed to gather in the forest was enough to keep me going, and it was enough to keep me from having an empty stomach. I walked for a very long time until I rather exhausted, resting at night in whatever enclosures I can find myself in around the warmth of a fire.

After several days of traveling I found myself in unfamiliar territory, but fortunately I hadn't come across any other people, members of enemy tribes who might do me harm. Occasionally I saw some people off in the distance and managed to hide, but luckily nobody bothered me. The fact that I was able to evade detection by so many people repeatedly was making me feel that I was better at this than I thought.

As the days grew warmer I didn't even mind the fact that I was going around completely naked, there was a certain feeling of freedom in that. I had always preferred spending time alone in nature to being around others all the time, and although I occasionally did feel lonely, having been alone for the first time out in the open and exposed like that felt especially freeing.

For the first time in my life I was truly on my own and it actually wasn't a very bad feeling. There was certain peacefulness to being alone in nature, to being unencumbered by anything, including the clothes on my back. Occasionally I did wonder what Angry Elk had done with my clothing, and thought that maybe I should have looked for it better before I left, although I did leave in kind of a rush, for understandable reasons.

I began laughing to myself as I thought of him tearing up my clothing, even burning it and shouting my name. I did occasionally wonder to myself how he was faring without me. I am sure that he probably found others who would suit his needs. I well knew that he didn't have any trouble finding women to gratify him, although I felt bad for the women who thought that he was worth gratifying. But he was their problem now, and I was free of him and I had no intention of going back.

"Let the bastard starve or die of infection for all I care," I said as I began laughing to myself. For a moment I felt like I was being cruel, or excessively vindictive, but every time I felt guilty over my actions I reminded myself just how badly he had treated me and the guilt went away.

The way I saw that he was a big boy and could take care of himself, and if he couldn't that was his problem, I wasn't there to be his slave or his sex toy, now I was free, and I didn't feel I needed anybody. I didn't need a man to take care of me, and I didn't need one for companionship either, all I needed now for companionship was nature all around me.

I continued walking for many more days in a fairly predictable pattern that soon became a regular rhythm. I would walk for several hours, stopping along the way to gather whatever food that I could and eating it along the way. Then towards the end of the day I would go to the nearby stream and I would catch some fish so that I could eat something more substantial. I would also replenish myself in the water and would also bathe to get the sweat off of my body and to keep me cool during the warm days.

As the sun began setting I would try to find shelter for myself, and using the wood that I had gathered throughout the day I would start a fire that would hopefully keep me warm throughout the night.

After I had traveled further than I ever had before, beyond any recognizable place that I could put my finger on, I wondered how far I was going to go, was I just going to keep going forever, never to rest?

I shrugged my shoulders. It was a weird thought that I had just abandoned civilization altogether, but at the same time I had never been happier. Although I occasionally wondered what my family would have thought when they discovered that I was missing, and I occasionally missed the time I spent with Sprinting Rabbit, I guess I always was a solitary individual at heart. It really was true that I preferred spending time in nature to spending time with people, and it seemed like it suited me well.

I still couldn't picture the idea that I would never see civilization again. I felt that at some point I would desire human companionship again, just to hear the voice of another human being and to interact with them, but for the time being the sound of the birds chirping and the other sounds of the forest were companionship enough for me, and I felt content with that.

After a few weeks of travel I was noticing another interesting thing, my solitude and my isolation from the world were making me feel not just a deeper connection to nature, but I felt like I was having a greater connection to the great spirits around me. As I had gone without human contact I was noticing the behavior of animals more, finding their behavior even more predictable, like I could almost communicate with them, like I had felt a oneness with nature and all the spirits of the forest around me.

At night my dreams were incredibly vivid and I almost felt as though I were leaving my body. I felt like I had become an animal at night, prowling through the forest, like I was mentally connected to the animals of the forest, like I could understand the sound of the chirping of the crickets and the howling of the wolves and all the other noises of wildlife.

My dreams were powerful and lucid, and all I saw were animals. Occasionally I would dream of my life back in the village, but as I spent more time out in the wilderness I found that people were fading not just from my waking thoughts, but also from my dreams as well, which were soon populated by animals and what I felt were the spirits of the animals.

In my dreams I could feel the animals speaking to me, giving me guidance, keeping me companionship. For a while I thought that maybe I was just longing for human contact again, but the more I thought of it the more I was finding myself happy and content to be alone among the animals.

One day however I realized that nature was sometimes less than forgiving and more hostile than I had remembered. Maybe it's because I hadn't bathed in a while, but I was finding my skin especially itchy, especially my back, and it was driving me positively mad.

I tried in vain to scratch my own back but I could not reach. I had remembered sometimes when my back had been really itchy in the past that I would have someone like Sprinting Rabbit who was kind enough to scratch it for me, and how much pleasure that gave me, but now I had no such assistance.

Eventually I found a tree which looked like it had thick bark on it and I started rubbing my back up against it in order to scratch my back. The pleasure I felt just to have that one carnal need satisfied was how I imagined Angry Elk had felt all the times I had gratified his many needs. This was a much simpler need, but having it met like that was satisfying beyond imagination.

However as the sensation of itchiness in my back finally started going away I suddenly started feeling a less pleasant sensation of stinging on my flesh. I started swatting at the areas where I felt the stinging and biting sensations and that was when I was realizing that all around me I was being stung by bees.

I started to shout and scream out in pain, and that was when I realized that my scratching my back against the tree had disturbed a bees nest, and now they were all swarming out after me.

I tried to swat the bees away but I realized that there were more of them that I could take, and I soon started running as they started chasing after me. The painful stinging sensation on my skin became intolerable and I knew that I had to seek shelter somewhere. I continued running as fast as I could until finally I had seen a river and I jumped into it until the water had become deep enough that I could go underneath the water. I kept going underneath the water for as long as I could hold my breath as I swam downstream. Eventually I got far enough away that I had successfully escaped from the bees.

After swimming down the stream for a while, convinced that the bees had finally left me alone, I got myself out of the water and started trying to dry off. I looked at my skin and I could see that there were welts from the bees all over me and that I was going to be swelling up soon.

I eventually found some shelter and started picking all of the stingers out of my flesh, painfully as my body swelled up with the bee venom. I was feeling too lousy that night to even eat anything or try to look for food and I figured I would need a day of rest.

As I went to sleep in my cave that night all I could think to myself is that while I still enjoyed nature, and I still liked the animals, but I did not feel so similarly inclined towards the insects anymore.

11

I soon recovered from my unfortunate encounter with the

smaller aspects of nature that I didn't quite like. I had always hated bees from a young age, now I was positively terrified of them. I would never scratch my back against a tree without carefully surveying it first, I wouldn't make that mistake again.

I stayed sore for a little while from my bee stings, and over time I healed from them, but found myself feeling a little bit less than spectacular. At first I attributed to the fact that I had been walking and traveling for a very long time and had been very physically active lately. But then I noticed that I began having strange cravings for foods that I found myself unable to obtain in the forest.

After a couple more days I found myself vomiting every morning and feeling nauseous. I briefly thought to myself that maybe it was some type of reaction to my encounter with the bees several days before, but finally it occurred to me. I remembered that my mother and grandmother had told me that when they were pregnant they experienced all sorts of sickness in the morning from it.

That was when I realized another thing, since I had taken my leave from the village I realized that I had not been inconvenienced by my monthly flow of blood. I had heard that sometimes when you were physically active that could delay your cycle, but my cycles tended to be very regular, and now I realized I had not had one this entire time and the terrible truth dawned on me.

"I must be pregnant," I said to myself one day as I felt my stomach, once again feeling sick, and not just from the morning sickness that my mother had told me about, but sick to have thought that this was one more thing from Angry Elk that I did not want.

As this realization dawned on me, for a moment I

felt extremely infuriated. Angry Elk with his constant need for sexual gratification must have gotten me pregnant, and in all of my anger and fury at him during that time I hadn't even realized the signs of this. Now I had something growing inside of me that I did not know how to deal with.

It was not that I didn't like the idea of children, I always enjoyed spending time with my brothers and sisters, but I guess in my naïveté I had never considered the consequences of gratifying all of my husband's needs. It had never even occurred to me that I might someday be pregnant like that, let alone so soon, but then when I was with Angry Elk the sexual encounters were extremely frequent, so I guess I should have expected as much, but now it caught me off of guard and I didn't know how to deal with it.

Surely I could not care for a child out in the middle of the woods by myself. I didn't know the first thing about caring for a baby or even how to give birth to a baby. I knew that after a woman gave birth she was sometimes incapacitated for a while, and that sometimes a woman could even die from the process.

When I considered that I suddenly became very afraid. Now here I was out in the middle of nowhere completely by myself facing the possibility of giving birth to a child that I did not know how to take care of, and I did not know if it would end up killing me.

At that moment panic set in, and for a while I thought that maybe I should start heading back to the village. I could deal with a lot of things on my own, but I felt like a baby growing inside of me was something that I needed help with, something that others would have to help me with if I wanted to survive the process.

I tried to think to myself how far along I might have

been. It had been several weeks since I had had my cycle, and I had only been noticing these symptoms of sickness and nausea more recently. I figured that I must have been pregnant for at least a couple of weeks, or maybe even a few months at this point, it only becoming noticeable just recently, so I figured I had several months before the child was due to be born, my stomach didn't even expand that much yet, as much as Angry Elk had always complained that I was fat, I certainly didn't notice a tremendous amount of weight gain.

I shook my head though. There was no way I could go back to the village after having been gone for so long. There was also no way that if I was going to have a child that I was going to allow that child to be subjected to the abuses of my husband. If I was going to have a child I was going to keep it safe from the likes of him.

I suppose it was possible that I could always give birth to the child and then leave it outside of a village and somebody would find it and take care of it, but that was if I survived the process of the birth itself. Although several women in the village had given birth I had never witnessed it before, and I was told that it was often very painful. The thought that it could even kill me was extremely frightening to me, as it sounded like a cruel and painful way to die.

Over the next couple of days I tried to not think about it as much, tried to go about my daily routine and get back into my normal rhythm, but every day I knew that the baby was growing larger inside of me, making me hungrier, draining my life force.

I found I was able to deal with the nausea and the morning sickness, and luckily it wasn't affecting my ability to take care of myself, but I knew that towards the later stages of pregnancy it would become extremely difficult for me to survive out in the forest on my own. I needed to start thinking about what I was going to do in the long term about the growing problem inside of me.

As time went on I was finding that the nausea and the morning sickness were getting even worse, until one day as I was walking through the forest I suddenly realized that I was bleeding and felt an intense pain coming out of me.

"No, it's too soon," I said at the thought that I might be giving birth at the moment. However I did not seem to be giving birth, I just seem to be bleeding a lot, bleeding a lot for the first time since I noticed the unexpected end of my cycles, and as I did so I found myself feeling increasingly weak.

As I started to expel a large amount of blood from my body I thought that maybe this was it, I was going to die from this, I was going to die giving birth, perhaps as a punishment for abandoning my husband. I prayed to the great spirit for forgiveness, said to myself that I was sorry for abandoning everything that I knew, except when I thought to myself more deeply I realized that I did not mean it.

With what little strength I had left I moved over to the nearby river and started washing myself off of all the blood and drinking more to replenish all of the fluids that I was losing. But I was finding myself feeling dizzy, so I quickly got out of the water, took a few steps away and that was when I collapsed.

12

I don't know how long I had passed out for, but when I came to I felt somebody poking me and shouting something to me in a language or dialect that I didn't understand, and in an accent that was unfamiliar to me.

I still felt too weak to get up of my own accord, but as I looked up I found myself surrounded by a woman who was shaking me and shouting something that to me. I couldn't understand what she was saying but it looked like she was concerned for me, so I pointed to my stomach and held my stomach as though I were in pain, which I was.

I then I reluctantly pointed between my legs and I could see that I was once again bleeding as she nodded, seeming to understand what was going on. She started shouting something else and some of her companions came by. She said something to me that I still didn't understand but she was pointing off in the distance, and I took it to mean that she was going to go get help for me.

She started running off as her other companions stayed there with me, and a couple of them held me by the hand. I wasn't sure if this is what dying was like, but I certainly felt weak and rather sick. It didn't look like I gave birth but it looked like whatever was growing inside of me had come out, one way or another.

A short while later a couple of people came back, and some of the men from her tribe picked me up and they slowly carried me back to their village and into a house where they put me down on some animal skins. By that time I was feeling rather feverish and felt embarrassed as I felt myself vomiting on their clean floor.

A man came into the room dressed as though he were a shaman. Much like the other villagers I couldn't quite understand what he was saying, but it looked like he was saying some type of ceremonial prayer for me as he took some type of a rag and pressed it against my forehead.

A woman at my side held my hand and squeezed it tight and seemed to realize what I was going through. It was then that I realized that I must have lost the baby, along with a lot of blood, and I was still feeling afraid that I wasn't going to pull through.

Eventually I fell asleep and when I woke up it was rather late and I could see that there was a roaring fire inside of the house. The fire felt nice and warm, and I wanted to say something to the people who had brought me there. The woman who had initially found me was sitting by my side and seemed to be smiling as she saw that I woke up.

"Thank you," I said, and although they couldn't understand my language I felt that they understood what the meaning was. I started pointing to my chest and my heart area. "Thank you from the bottom of my heart."

The woman went over and brought me a bowl with some water in it that I drank up greedily and it felt extremely refreshing. I felt like I was most likely dehydrated, I felt powerfully thirsty and still extremely weak, and she continued to sit there pressing something against my forehead and waiting for my fever to go down.

I soon fell back asleep but then I woke up the next morning and I gave a silent prayer to the Great Spirit that I was still alive. During the night I had had a lot of experiences, had seen a lot of things that seemed rather strange to me, maybe I was hallucinating, maybe I was having a spiritual vision of some kind, but I felt that the spirit of the child that was going to be growing inside of me had departed and that it bore me no hard feelings.

My host seemed pleased with the fact that I was doing better in the morning, and they brought me some type of breakfast, some type of soup, something that was easy to digest. They probably figured that after everything I had gone through I had better start recovering slowly and better not take things too fast.

I once again nodded and thanked them, pointing to my chest, as I felt that it was a way of indicating that I was grateful for the food as I rubbed my stomach and smiled.

I had to admit that feeling so helpless and being cared for by others was making me feel like I was a burden to them, and made me feel that maybe my flight from civilization was shortsighted, and that maybe I couldn't really cut it on my own. I had been doing so well for so many weeks, but after an incident like this I realized that there are some situations in which you do need the rely on the help and well-being of others.

I wished that I could communicate better with my hosts but they seemed friendly enough. The shaman came by once or twice a day to give me some kind of medicine and say some prayers, for which I was grateful, as whatever he was giving me was making me feel better.

I did feel somewhat bad that I had realized that I had lost my child, even though I didn't feel I was up to raising a child, it was still sad to think that I had gone through all of that for nothing. In fact after that experience I never wanted to go through something like that again. As far as I was concerned I never needed to be with another man for the rest of my life.

For the next few days I found myself in a new routine where I would spend much of my time resting and sleeping as these people nursed me back to health and fed me until I had regained my strength. Over the course of time we started to learn some of each other's language, and I realized that the woman who saved me was named Blooming Flower, which seemed to suit her personality, as she was a cheerful and upbeat individual and seemed to be rather affectionate towards me, unusually so.

After a few days I started to realize that her affection for me was more than just her being friendly, I felt that she was actually starting to fall in love with me. I had never been with a woman before in the same sense that I had been with Angry Elk, but Blooming Flower was very gentle towards me, unlike the way he was. It was nice for a change to be shown such affection by another human being.

I didn't know how long I was expected to stay with these people, I felt like I didn't want to be imposing on them for very long, but Blooming Flower kept repeatedly insisting that I should stay because I might still need to rely on their help at some point in the future. I felt like she had ulterior motives for having me stay, as she was clearly very impressed by me, which admittedly was flattering if somewhat awkward.

However I felt that she had a point, and it was getting towards that colder part of the year, so I figured it couldn't hurt to stay with her for a while. It was actually quite nice to be around people again, at least among people who treated me nicely, even if I didn't fully understand their language, I could understand that they were kind people, as that was a quality that transcended language.

As I regained my strength I started to help around the house more with cooking and cleaning, but unlike with Angry Elk they were not demanding that I do anything, and frequently seemed to think that I should take my rest, but I didn't want to be a burden to them and wanted to help out as much as possible, and soon it felt good to be among other people and socializing with them again.

I think that Blooming Flower was a little bit

disappointed when I started wearing clothing again! It soon became clear to me that around the village she was a little bit seen as eccentric, for she clearly preferred the company of women in an intimate sense.

I had never been with a woman like that before, but I did feel close to her and I felt like I owed her something. So one night while we were together and alone she slowly and carefully started approaching me before kissing me on the lips and soon we found ourselves in bed together. It was weird being with another woman, I had never been intimate like this with another woman, not even with Sprinting Rabbit, but Sprinting Rabbit very much preferred the company of men, at least in the intimate sense, even abusive men like Angry Elk. But at least being with a woman there was no chance that she would put another child inside of me that would endanger my life.

I found that Blooming Flower was a very tender and affectionate lover, in contrast to my former husband, but still something felt weird about being with her like that. Clearly she very much wanted me to stay, but I couldn't help but think of what was happening back in my village. Although I didn't really intend to return there I did miss my family and I did miss my friends, even if I was something of a solitary individual at heart.

That was why one night, after careful contemplation, I decided it was time for me to once again set out on my own. I felt bad at the idea of leaving my hosts like that after all they had done for me, but I realized that I could not stay there forever, I was an outsider and I did not fully belong there.

Before leaving however I kissed my fingers and placed my fingers on Blooming Flower's forehead and waved her goodbye. She could see me leaving and she looked sad to see me go, but I think that she understood it was not meant to be, I had to go where the winds happened to carry me, even if I didn't know quite where that would be or where it would take me.

13

I realized as I set out on my journey again in the colder season that maybe I should have stayed in the village with Blooming Flower, at least there I would have been warm and taken care of and have a place to go to every night, but something compelled me to keep traveling. I didn't know where I was traveling to, but I just felt like I had some compulsive need to continue traveling.

I wasn't sure if it was the spirits of the forest that were driving me on, or the spirits of my ancestors, or my own stubborn nature, but something about being alone and out in the elements appealed to me even when the weather started getting rougher.

As I traveled further and further from my original point of origin, I now realized that I was very far from the place of my birth, and that I probably wouldn't be able to find my way back even if I tried. For the most part I kept to myself and I avoided any type of civilization. Occasionally I would see signs of people but I would always hide. Somehow I had developed an aversion to civilization in general.

I didn't know if I would ever go back to civilization again, but I knew that I couldn't spend too much time there before I got restless. I was now in a strange and new land among people whose languages I did not speak and whose customs were foreign to me. To a large degree I didn't feel like I fully fit in anywhere, maybe I really did just belong alone and on my own.

Occasionally when I was out taking refuge from the cold I missed the companionship of Sprinting Rabbit, or even the more intimate contact that I had with Blooming Flower, but a continuing restlessness drove me on as I continued traveling further and further.

However as time continued I found myself growing exhausted of the constant motion, of never settling in one place. And as the cold season came in I was finding the food was becoming scarcer. At least when I had been back in the village of my birth we always tended to have a good harvest, and the hunters always brought back a good amount of food, but I knew that out there most people weren't as lucky as we were, and now I was starting to learn that the hard way.

There were days when I didn't have anything to eat or I only had the minimal amount to eat. During this time of year the food wasn't growing as much, although I could always still rely on fish as a form of sustenance. However in the cold of winter I didn't enjoy as much standing in the cold of the water, and I soon found myself coming down with a cold and spending more time taking refuge from the elements.

One day, after several days without food, I was realizing my situation was getting rather desperate, and I needed to find something that could sustain me for a while, perhaps even for several days or several weeks. Although I had fished and gathered for most of my food, I wasn't that much of a hunter, not in the way that Angry Elk was. At least he always managed to provide enough food, but I would rather my stomach be empty than my freedom restricted by the likes of him any day.

I knew that if I wanted food that would last me for a while during this time when a lot of animals were hibernating, I would have to find myself a deer. A deer would provide me with enough meat to last me for a long stretch of time, but I wasn't exactly sure how to hunt one.

I did know a little bit about tracking from what I had picked up from Angry Elk and the other hunters, but I was certainly no expert, and I had never tried hunting on my own before. I was also not sure exactly what I was going to use to take down my target, as stabbing it with a knife didn't seem like a realistic option because I would need to get too close to make it practical.

I decided the best bet would be using a pointed and sharpened stick as a way of spearing it, and then I could use the knife to skin the carcass and separate the meat, and perhaps also use the skin as a way of keeping myself warmer in the increasingly cold weather.

It took me a long time to find any deer that I felt would be sufficient, and then I slowly approached my target. I knew that I had to be very quiet as I didn't want to risk startling it. However when I knew it was time to throw the spear I knew that I had to try to drive it out, so I started running towards it with the spear, which unfortunately seemed to just startle it and it came charging right at me. I tried throwing the spear at it, but unfortunately I missed and collided directly with the deer which sent me flying.

I ended up falling right into the water and I felt an excruciating pain in my chest. It took me for a moment to recover my equilibrium, but I soon managed to keep myself from drowning and pulled myself out of the water. I tried standing up but the pain in my chest was agonizing and I was finding that I was having trouble breathing.

At first I thought it was just the shock of the freezing water that had been a shock to my system, but now I realized that the pain in my chest wasn't going away, and that every breath I took I felt a stabbing sensation in my chest. I put my fingers in my mouth and that was when I realized that there was blood in my mouth.

I slowly made my way over to a tree and I leaned against it for support and slowly sat down and rested as I tried harder to breathe. However with each breath that I took I found that the pain was increasing and I could taste more blood in my mouth, to the point where it felt like I was choking on it.

I felt my chest and pressed down on it, and that was when I realized I must have broken a bone, and that bone most likely had punctured something and was making it difficult for me to breathe. I wanted to call out for help, but I didn't know of anyone who was nearby. I couldn't remember the last time I had seen an inhabited village, and being barely able to stand up I knew there was no way that I could walk to another village in this state.

I struggled to breathe as I wrapped my arms around myself and tried to keep warm. But between the cold and the pain in my chest I was finding it very hard to stay focused. I decided that I would try some breathing exercises, but with each breath I took I continued to struggle to catch my breath, as I found it harder and harder to breathe with myself increasingly choking on blood by the minute.

Touching my chest I could see that I was bleeding from that area as well, and I could feel like bone was poking out. I was injured and I was injured badly, my only hope was that somebody would come along and find me, maybe some caring soul like Blooming Flower.

As I started gasping increasingly with each breath I thought to myself that she had quite a beautiful name, the thought of a blooming flower made me think of spring, of summer, of the warmth of the sun on my naked skin. As I thought of that I imagine myself running naked through the forest, the warm feeling of the sun invigorating me, and I started to feel warmth spreading through my body.

The warm feeling continued to grow throughout my body as my breath grew more and more infrequent and I was having a harder time swallowing. But the warm feeling continued and soon it was enveloping my whole body, it was calling to me, it was a gentle feeling that was embracing me, and very reluctantly I gave in, closed my eyes and smiled as I slipped away from the world for the final time.

Epilogue

As I surrendered myself to the warm feeling around me I soon found myself surrounded in light, surrounded by all of the spirits of nature who were calling to me and embracing me with open arms, they were there to welcome me to my home with the great spirit in the sky.

There was a feeling of love and acceptance, a feeling of warmth as all of the cold and the pain that I have been feeling moments earlier dissipated around me, and it seemed like the pain and the cold of that moment were a distant bad dream, and that I found myself in a place where there was no cold and there was no pain.

I could find myself bathed in the warm light and I could feel that it was calling to me, calling me to go home, for that was where I truly belonged.

For a moment I hesitated, and I thought of all the people that I would be leaving behind who I had met on my journey. As I embraced the warmth I felt a sense of forgiveness towards everybody, even towards Angry Elk.

As I floated there, looking down on my cold and

motionless body under the tree, I saw the winter turned to spring and I saw people come to bury my body. As I floated above the world I looked it over all the villages that I had come across, I finally returned back to my village, even if just to say goodbye, to my mother and father, to my grandparents, to my brothers and sisters and to Sprinting Rabbit.

As I moved away from all of that and found myself walking towards a waterfall, the very waterfall that bore my name, I heard it singing to me and the song that it was singing was the song that was, at long last, calling me to my true home.

It was warm there and nothing hurt.

Author Notes

I always try to write something at the end of everything that I write about what inspired the story and what I was trying to achieve with it. In this case it was directly inspired by past life memories I have had of a particular Native American lifetime going back nearly 20 years. Initially I only had a few memories of this lifetime over the years but it kept coming back to me.

The initial memory I had of this lifetime was a memory where I was head-butted by some deer and getting hurt badly. I think I managed to escape by diving into a stream but it was winter so the stream was freezing cold. I managed to swim to the other side but I got sick from cold as well as from injuries from the deer attack. I sat under a tree in pain and then fell asleep and died.

Later on I had more memories that I associated with this particular lifetime such as another memory where I saw a bunch of women with giant baskets on their back carrying some type of stalks of some type of a crop that might have been corn that was sticking out of the baskets on their backs, and it looks like they were in front of some type of a field full of similar stalks.

The next memory that I had I saw myself as a naked Native American woman rubbing my back against a tree in order to scratch myself, and I felt that at one point in that lifetime I was attacked by a swarm of bees and badly stung, which is consistent with my phobia in this life of bees or bees nests, just seeing one of those things is enough to give me a panic attack practically.

It's kind of hard to place that life, but I feel it might have been in Mississippi or something like that in pre-Columbian era. This is a life I remember vividly from time to time because it was an unusual life where I seemed to live in an entirely solitary existence where I didn't even wear clothing and had no communication with other human beings, and was very much in touch with nature, which again just reflects a strong pattern of solitude in many lifetimes, but this one even stronger than most.

I did have one other memory that I originally thought was associated with this lifetime and when I was looking up stuff about the Native Americans in Mississippi and everything like that I found this image of what apparently was human sacrifice of 53 women that took place in that particular culture, and it looked exactly like something I had seen in a vision previously, so I am wondering if it somehow relates to that particular life or if maybe that was another life altogether later on.

These were the main memories I had of this life over the course of 20 years. I felt it was a mostly uneventful lifetime but it's one that obviously I think had a strong effect on me, because even though I only had a few memories of this life they came back to me very frequently, showing many themes from a lot of the past lives I recall of solitary existence and retreating from society, with this one being a more extreme case.

Finally in November 2021 I decided to do a regression to get more information on this lifetime and work out the details with the intention of fully turning everything that I recalled into a novel or a novella of some kind, which would be my second past life autobiography after my first book on the topic, People of the Icy Tundra, which is also about my past lives as a Native American during the Ice Age.

Prior to doing the regression to this particular lifetime I was thinking that in general I had a happy life until I was married to somebody who basically raped me, and then I sort of ran away from civilization and I think I went around mostly naked encountering people only from time to time. I feel like I eventually got sick from the cold weather and that at one point I ended up being attacked by bees. For a while I thought maybe I gave birth or something like that, but I'm pretty sure that aside from that one sexual encounter I mostly avoided people, although I think I might have gone from villages from time to time and I might have had a relationship with a woman in that lifetime.

But ultimately I remembered that I died through being hit by some type of animal and suffering injuries and dying from that and I even looked that up in my past life memories document. Apparently I didn't have that one added to the past life biographies document, but I do recall that I had memories of that lifetime just randomly. I also felt my name might have been Singing Waterfall and I thought that maybe I could make a novella out of that.

Eventually I did the following regression on my own

one November night and this is what emerged that gave clarity to all of the details of my past life that I had been recalling in fragments over the last 20 years or so. It was this regression that formed pretty much the basis for the entire novella.

(Regression: Pre-Columbian Native American Woman in Late Woodland Period Mississippi Culture): I decided to do a regression tonight because I wanted to learn more about this past life that I had been aware of for a long time but never really explored more deeply, but mostly because I felt like if I explored them more deeply I could maybe write a novella about it, so I took that small file that's only like 23 minutes long on YouTube and was able to have a pretty good regression experience using it. This was my first regression since way back in February 2021 now, so I really hadn't done one in a while.

The regression file starts by trying to relax you but even before it started I was getting all of these impressions of being in a Native American village with all of these beating drums, and everybody was dancing around, and I felt that this was a very communal event where we were all dancing around to commune with nature in some way and everything like that. I also felt myself eating some type of a fruit or vegetable like a squash that I remembered biting into and I seem to be enjoying it, even though that's not a food that I currently enjoy in my current life.

I could really feel my body and what it felt like in contrast to my current life. I felt myself kneeling and I could feel my legs and I had long hair and everything like that, and felt I had reasonably average sized breasts or maybe a little bit large, I just felt the difference from my current day male body though very distinctly. I also felt that I had tattoos on my face and arm, geometric patterns mostly I think, but I wasn't really sure specifically what they look like.

Then it started asking me what I looked like explicitly and asked me to look down at my feet, and I felt that I had moccasins at one point but that most of the time I preferred to go barefoot. But I got the sense that I was considered to be relatively attractive and everything like that, I felt my body was delicate but strong, really feminine but resilient and physically fit and everything like that, in contrast to my current life body.

It told me to look around at my surroundings and I see myself in a small village, and it seemed like it was surrounded by forests and lots of trees in every single direction, and that houses were made of wood for the most part, as well as tree bark and things like that. I could see that there were lots of children running around the village and it felt like I had a peaceful happy life there. I felt it was a very festive society in general; like that there were a lot of festivals and holidays and everything like that. I saw lots of family members and men and women, and I remember that I was looking after a lot of young children like siblings, and I really seemed to like children a lot in that life in contrast to my current life.

I got the sense that I was very physical in that life and that it was a very warm area and sunny, and that and I spent a tremendous amount of time out alone in the woods and everything. I felt that I knew a lot about plants and animals, and that I spent a lot of time in the forest gathering food and plants, both for food and medicine and things like that. I think I spent more time alone in the forest by myself than I did in the village and liked to spend a lot of time in solitude, even though I still seemed more social than I was in this life, seeing as I seem to be festive and celebrating with lots of children and everything all the time, and that I liked to go skinny dipping in swimming naked in the river.

It asked me what my name was and I felt it was something like Segna, which I felt meant singing waterfall, because I think that I liked the sound of the waterfall or it had something to do with my birth or something like that. I felt this was in the Mississippi area near Arkansas, perhaps near the border, incidentally where I recall living in the first part of my 1800s lifetime involving the Trail of Tears, which is another past life of mine that I hope to turn into a novel length past life autobiography one day, with this one being the interesting prequel I suppose.

When it asked me what my purpose was in that lifetime I said that I felt it was to find some type of a balance between communicating with people and being solitary and by myself, and it seemed like I actually had a pretty good balance, seeing as I seem to have a more active social life interacting with people and active in the village, even though I still felt I spent a large amount of time out in the forest by myself in solitude with nature.

It asked me to go to a major event and it brought me to what I felt like was my marriage to a man that I didn't know very well, and I felt I was sort of an eligible bachelorette at seeing as I was considered to be attractive and everything like that. The guy that I married I felt was sort of like a big person around town, and maybe sort of a strong hunter or warrior or something along those lines. I got the sense that he was very muscular and had lots of scars all over his body and was a very large person in general, although again I felt apprehensive about marrying him as I didn't really know him very well and it felt like more of an arranged type of marriage.

I felt that we lived together in a house that had sort of a wooden top made of wood and the floor, and some of the walls were made of dirt. After marrying him I felt like things got bad fast, as I felt that he was extremely sexual and very aggressive, but he was very domineering sexually and everything like that, and that he was physically abusive to me in general, and was very controlling and jealous. He didn't like me leaving and to go spend time off by myself outdoors and I don't think that he likes me being around other men or talking with other people. So he seemed like he was majorly restricting my freedom and was a very controlling and jerkish asshole in general, sort of one of those violent Alpha males with toxic masculinity. But I still felt like he was maybe respected around the village, like I said again he was sort of like a respected hunter and warrior or something along that, and was probably considered a highly eligible man on virtue of his strength.

After living with him for a short time I felt that I start to really truly hate him and I consider trying to kill him while he is sleeping, but then when I go to stab him I lose my resolve and can't bring myself to murder him in spite of all that. I then run away into the forest and decide that I will never return because I did not feel safe wherever I happen to be living. I felt like leaving him felt selfish at the same time, but I did seriously want to kill him, so I felt the fact that I just left and spared his life was sort of redeeming.

I think that I maybe only told one woman in the village where I was going, and I think that I spend a lot of time in the forest, literally running around buck naked and living like a wild person I guess. For my spontaneous memories I felt at one point I ended up getting stung by a nest of bees or something like that, but for the most part I survived in the forest just gathering food, and maybe hunting and fishing, but was very independent and lived a solitary life by myself.

I felt like maybe around the winter season I ended up going to another village or I came across a different village somewhere elsewhere in the world or that I traveled far from where I initially was born. I felt that I lived for a while in a village and I pursued some type of a lesbian relationship with another woman, or at least I was very close to another woman for a while, but I eventually left her as well to go back and pursue my solitary existence in the woods.

I felt that I died at a relatively young age where I was hunting in the forest, and I think that a deer sort of rammed into me and broke one of my ribs and I think it punctured my lung. It seemed like I actually hurt myself pretty badly and was having trouble breathing, but being alone living in the forest by myself I didn't really have anybody who could help me, so eventually I just sat down by a tree and then I feel that I eventually died of suffocation or choking on blood from the punctured lung. I felt eventually somebody came and found my body and buried it, but I felt like they didn't know who I was and that people didn't really know what became of me ultimately.

So overall it was a pretty interesting regression, and at least now I learned more about this life that I recalled many years ago but never explored more deeply until now, as I thought it might make for an interesting story to write around Thanksgiving time, even though other than the Native American aspect it has nothing to do with Thanksgiving, but I thought it would be a good idea to learn more about this life and maybe write a novella about it like I did with my Ice Age past lives.

It did seem like it started out as a very happy life but then after being abused by my husband I seem to have left and avoided people after that, except for that one woman I grew close to. But it seemed like after that I didn't really trust men as much in that lifetime and pursued a solitary existence for the most part before eventually dying, since I had nobody else to help me when I was injured. So I guess the overall theme of that life that came up in the regression was fairly accurate, it seems like that whole life was sort of a push and pull between interacting with other people and being alone and independent by myself in the forest. It seemed like a somewhat lonely life, but I felt like I preferred being by myself, much like I do in my current life and it was occasionally I would go to other villages and interact with people but then I would move on.

I later tried to research this on the Internet and although I didn't get a specific year range for this life I felt that it was a short life where I probably died in my late teens or early 20s, and I felt that I lived sometime in the Mississippian culture in what is known as the late Woodland period taking place between 1000 and 1500 years ago, a time when there was a transition between the small hunter gatherer tribes and villages and these larger more urban societies of mound builders.

Just looking at it in general it does seem like the homes that I saw in my regression match up with depictions that I found on the Internet of what dwellings looked like in that time and place. It looked like it was mostly a tribe of hunters and gatherers but they still started settling and farming more, and I seem to be more of a gatherer than a farmer. I do recall eating squash, which was one of the major three staples of food that they grew in that time and place, so that was accurate as well, and it seemed like there were lots of small distinct cultures of their own, which is consistent with the fact that I remember journeying around from village to village, each with their own sort of distinct society I guess you would say.

It also suggested that there was hunting with bows and arrows and spears and stuff like that, hunting large game and everything like that until the populations were decimated, and it seemed common for them to hunt deer, so it does seem like that's probably what ultimately ended up killing me. I was most likely hunting that deer and it happened to ram into me in self-defense breaking my rib, and since there was no one around to help me I eventually died from that injury, where as if I had lived in a village perhaps I would have survived.

So again I didn't really read a tremendous amount about it but it does seem like everything that I recall in my regression is pretty consistent and historically accurate with the late Woodland period of Mississippian Native American culture sometime between 500-1000 A.D.

I have always found reincarnation to be interesting because it explains so many things about one person's current life and why we are all unique individuals. Traditional materialism would suggest that we were blank slates at birth, but when you look at even very young children they have interests and abilities and talents that seem to be inherently inborn. When you look at even a young child they do not seem to be much of a blank slate as we would assume.

I think it is quite common for children to remember past lives, and when I was younger I was always interested in Native American cultures and still am to this day. I feel that forgetting past lives in most cases is a natural process, even though some retain the memory into adulthood. After reading a lot about current life memory and how current life memories work, it's interesting to note that most people don't recall much of their life before the age of seven, and that by the age of seven we have lost most of our memories from before the age of three. So I am thinking that past life memories are something that is part of our childhood memories that in most cases just doesn't translate into adulthood, but always subconsciously is influencing us in some way.

Reincarnation is also interesting in that you can see what you would do if you're in a different time and place and situation. As a white male living in modern-day America it's a far cry from living as a Native American female in pre-Columbian times. Even though the setting and circumstances have changed I can see the similar personality still coming through, that tendency to retreat from conflict and from society seems to be a tendency that I have carried through many lifetimes, preferring freedom and solitude to large communities and social gatherings.

Although I always loved Native American culture from a young age I do remember one incident from when I was younger. I remember a Native American Princess visited our school, and as part of that they wanted us all to put face paint on our faces, and I remember that the idea of doing that really bothered me, and I think it could have been bringing up memories from this lifetime and other ones involving violence and war. Now in the context of past lives these unusual feelings in the current life make perfect sense.

One last thing that I would mention in closing is that

for many years now I have always had this postcard that I got at a store for Native American paraphernalia of a Native American woman sitting in front of a waterfall that I always liked, and after seeing this particular past life I can see why that particular card stood out for me and why I felt compelled to buy it as I felt that seeing it triggered memories of this lifetime on an unconscious level. Now I keep it on my table where I look at it each day and now as I do so I am reminded of this past life, which while sad at times, still also fills me with largely happy memories.

For more samples of my writing check out my blog at https://stephensipila.wordpress.com/ and follow me on twitter at https://twitter.com/StephenSipila.

Stephen Sipila

1/29/2022

9 7 9 8 8 3 9 8 5 6 8 1 3